SCHOOL DAYS

SCHOOL DAYS

A Novel

Jonathan Galassi

OTHER PRESS
NEW YORK

Production editor: Yvonne E. Cárdenas
Text designer: Jennifer Daddio / Bookmark Design & Media Inc.
This book was set in Bulmer MT
by Alpha Design & Composition of Pittsfield, NH

1 3 5 7 9 10 8 6 4 2

Library of Congress Cataloging-in-Publication Data
Names: Galassi, Jonathan, author.
Title: School days : a novel / Jonathan Galassi.
Description: New York : Other Press, [2022]
Identifiers: LCCN 2021039952 (print) | LCCN 2021039953 (ebook) |
ISBN 9781635421897 (hardcover) | ISBN 9781635421996 (ebook)
Subjects: LCGFT: Novels.
Classification: LCC PS3557.A387 S36 2022 (print) | LCC PS3557.A387 (ebook) |
DDC 813/.54—dc23
LC record available at https://lccn.loc.gov/2021039952
LC ebook record available at https://lccn.loc.gov/2021039953

For

TERRY SUMMERFIELD

and

TENOCH ESPARZA

the voice in my head said

LOVE IS THE DISTANCE
BETWEEN YOU AND WHAT YOU LOVE

—FRANK BIDART

PRINCIPAL CHARACTERS

The Leverett School, Leverett, Connecticut, 1964–2019

The 2000s

FACULTY

Boris Krohn, *Head of School*
Samuel Brandt, *English*
Dean Harris, *English*
Carla Van Ness, *English*

STUDENTS

Peter Reno, *Mount Vernon, New York*
Daphne Homans, *Cambridge, Massachusetts*
Abby Kumar, *Mill Valley, California*

The 1960s

FACULTY

Theodore Gibson, *English*

STUDENTS

Eddie Braddock, *Seattle, Washington*
Sam Brandt, *Hingham Massachusetts*
Ron Bryden, *Dallas, Texas*
Dave Darman, *Houston, Texas*
Ray Kaiser, *Phoenix, Arizona*
Sandy Pleyel, *New York, New York*
Johnny Pratt, *Shaker Heights, Ohio*

OCTOBER
2007

LATE AFTERNOON SUNLIGHT was flooding the apartment. Pillars of dust rotated in the drowsy air. He was glad to be home after a long day, ready to put his feet up and look at the paper, but the phone was vibrating in his jacket pocket.

He leaned back on the island in the kitchen and listened to the message from Jeanne Harrison, the Head's secretary. "Good afternoon, Sam," she enunciated crisply. "Boris would like to see you in his office at five o'clock."

The island was too big for the room. He and Anne had always got in each other's way when they cooked together, which they did if they couldn't face the dining hall. The pattern in the fake marble made it impossible to keep clean, since you couldn't see the dirt unless you were viewing it from the proper angle. But it wasn't their kitchen, after all. Leverett's head of facilities had radiated pride when he showed them the house after it had been rebuilt certified LEED-Gold. It was one hundred percent energy efficient and tight as a tick. The only way to let fresh air into the place was to open the door and fan it in. But the man was blind to how ugly his state-of-the-art remake of this ramshackle old New England farmhouse was. Bixler House, one of some forty residences in the town of Leverett that had been annexed for senior faculty and staff to live in once they'd done their twenty years of dorm duty, had been handsome in a shambling, peeling-paint, splintered way. Now the new windows were out of proportion and the kitchen-dining room with its pale linoleum floor belonged in a nursing home, as Anne put it. It looked institutional inside and out—which of course it was.

Sam took an apple from an old earthenware mixing bowl, nearly unreachable in the middle of the island. Everything was apple, apple, apple this time of year: apple cider, apple butter, apple crumble, applejack. Apples and pumpkins— and those twee little corn husk decorations everyone put up on their newly hung storm doors. Fall had a way of making him crabby, intolerant, restless in his skin, and prone to regret. Those sly, ever-shorter late October afternoons everyone professes to love were bound to bring on a disorienting queasiness. Emily Dickinson's "certain slant of light" was capable of really laying him low.

He had fifteen minutes before meeting Boris. He trudged upstairs to the rat's nest that was his study, threw his book bag on his desk, and fell into his old chintz reading chair. English 101 had been a slog. Afternoon classes often were, this early in the year, when the new arrivals were still getting their bearings. Convincing knobs, as freshmen were called, that what a character says in *Romeo and Juliet* doesn't necessarily reflect everything he or she is feeling wasn't as easy as you might think. The kids at this point were still clinging to the literal ways of reading they'd learned at home—if they'd read at all. His job was to unclog their mental pores, encourage them to stop repeating the commonplaces they'd parroted back to get them this far, and be willing to take the risk of being wrong. English, he'd always felt, was really about everything, other than mathematics. It took a term or two for most of them to understand that right and wrong wasn't the issue. Some never did; but inspiring that willingness to actually respond to what was there on the page lay at the heart of the vaunted Leverett way of teaching.

Sam brushed his hair, still more pepper than salt, he told himself—except when he saw the pewter-colored clippings on the barbershop floor. He straightened his tie before heading back downstairs. He could have used a shave and a clean shirt, too, but there wasn't time.

BORIS'S OFFICE WAS IN MAIN HALL on the north side of the Oval, the great lawn which School Street divides from the town green, with its Congregational church, yellow-brick library, historical society, and row of stately black-on-white Federal houses—just the way the center of one of Connecticut's oldest and most prosperous towns ought to look. To the north and east, the burnt-umber Halsey Hills lay low-slung beyond the invisible but still powerfully present Wachusett River, which rolls down from the mountains of northern Vermont through farmland still dotted here and there with old tobacco barns but otherwise largely swallowed up in the ticky-tack of suburbia. The school's stately acreage—emerald lawns flanked by stands of hardwood and traversed by the poky Leverett River—served up a picture postcard image of a bygone, idyllic New England. The school's forest-green flag, a golden hare embroidered in its center, flew just below the Stars and Stripes from the pole atop the neoclassical tower in the middle of the Oval, an exclamation point visible from almost everywhere on campus.

He'd spent more than half his life here. Four years of high school, back when it was still all boys, "where I got my education," he always said. Leverett is one of oldest, richest, and most academically distinguished high schools in the country. Classes took place in tutorial sessions of no more than ten or twelve. Students were encouraged, no, expected, to have ideas and defend them, which meant that Leverett boys—girls, too, for the past forty years—were famously articulate, at times insufferably so.

The name evokes old globes in firelit libraries, striped silk ties, stiff ancestral portraits, athletes with cleated shoes and muddy thighs. The sons of presidents had gone here, if not presidents themselves, senators, secretaries of state, scions of the robber barons and investment bankers who evolved into what passed for an American aristocracy— leavened more recently with the sons and daughters of aspirational professionals who wanted their children to hobnob with the Establishment. The school boasted relatively few artists or writers among its alumni, but it had always exuded an aura of meritocratic rather than purely pecuniary elitism. No one cares who you are when you come to Leverett, the saying went; it's who you become while you're here that counts. Meaning that you, too, if you kissed the rod, could be instilled with Leverett values, could dress, behave, think, and feel the Leverett way.

After Harvard—which was effectively more of the same— Sam had won a fellowship to Oxford, followed by an abortive year trying to stomach deconstruction as a graduate student at Duke. Then a dozen years teaching English at Hadley, Leverett's rival up north, before Mareike Crowley had called him home. And now he'd been here another two decades, nearly, trying to offer his students what the legendary masters, as they used to call them, of the previous generation had given him.

Sam loved teaching. True, the kids were unchanging, predictably fresh-faced and self-preoccupied while he and his peers grew ever hoarier and more crotchety. What kept him engaged was the hunger of some of them, their desire to take hold, to devour life whole, with the help of a well-timed nudge or two from their mentors. The moment when a student understands how a book makes its impact not frontally but by stealth, how it imperceptibly changes us, when it does, forever, was for him, as the saying goes, better than sex. He'd seen kids literally come alive, as had happened to him: slough off their families' need to shroud them in security and open themselves up to riskier ways of becoming themselves, at times with spectacular results. These were the achievements he was proudest of.

THE COOL THAT DESCENDS on an office once the workday is over had already fallen in Main. He met Jeanne, who'd been the assistant to five Leverett Heads, on her way out. She wore her hair short and frosted, and pink translucent glasses hung from a silver chain around her neck. Her Peter Pan blouse, trim A-line skirt, and no-nonsense flats conveyed a brisk self-possession.

Jeanne smiled and pointed him toward the inner sanctum. Boris was, as always, on the phone, with his feet up on the old partners' desk that had always struck Sam as too big for him. He covered his receiver and mouthed, "Afternoon!" as he went on with his conversation.

On or off the phone, Leverett's Head of School was invariably upbeat and down-to-earth. The alumni adored him, which meant he was always flying off to San Francisco or

Bangkok to woo donors and snow potential students, making friends as reliably as the green repp tie dotted with gold hares he invariably wore.

Sam had seen the photos of Boris and Lizzie when they were everybody's favorite young couple at Lawrenceville scattered in silver frames on side tables at the Head's residence: hair everywhere, the toothy smiles and glowing complexions of well-fucked young marrieds wreathed by a ring of rambunctious flaxen-haired children. Nowadays Boris was a little paunchy, with bags beneath his round black architect's glasses, and Lizzie had to be dyeing her straight-cut, dirty-blond hair. "She dresses like a guidance counselor," Anne used to say, which was a bit rich, given that that was her own profession. But how should Lizzie dress? Sam wondered. What was the appropriate uniform for a small-town New England lawyer married to the head of a leading private high school?

"What's up, boss?" Sam threw himself into one of the crewel-embroidered wing chairs facing Boris's desk and dangled a leg over one arm as Boris hung up the phone.

"We are! Ten points over last year in annual giving. And how about that football team! We're six and oh!"

"Well, hallelujah!"

Boris ignored Sam good-naturedly as he swiveled in his chair and looked out across the Oval, his fingers joined to form the usual church. He focused, a bit wanly Sam thought, then turned toward him. His owl-like face fell before he lifted his eyebrows, stretched his forehead, leaned forward, and stared into Sam's eyes.

"This is top secret. I know I can count on you."

Boris was masterful at appealing to Sam's loyalty in spite of what he knew was his boss's fundamental mistrust of him, and everyone else, no doubt. He'd always known that Boris was unreachable, but he'd never given up hope that he could somehow worm his way into his heart. Something visceral bound Sam to him, even if he understood Boris's weaknesses inside out—just as Boris knew his. Leverett's fearless leader was emphatically not an intellectual or an educational visionary, and he made no bones about it. What he was, was an incredibly effective cheerleader. And money-spinner. And tactician, if not strategist. Was Leverett the great school it had once been? Sam asked himself this self-lacerating question almost daily. Arguably not; it was softer, less certain of its mission, less single-minded in its pedagogy, and there were hallways-ful of administrators in Main who were interpreting Ephraim Leverett's Deed of Gift in ways that left the originalists among the Old Guard perpetually outraged. The students, too, were blander and more predictable: cookie-cutter achievers out to make an impression. But Leverett was also wealthier, better known, more diverse, more manicured, and harder to get into than it had ever been. Much of the credit went to Boris Krohn.

"Do you remember a student named Bryden, Ronald Bryden, class of '67? Your vintage if I'm not mistaken."

"Vaguely. I think we were in Latin one together."

"He didn't return after third year," Boris said, rifling through a pile of papers on his desk. "Any idea why?"

"None."

"I had an interesting missive from Ron Bryden yesterday." He handed it over, pursing his lips while he watched Sam read.

3478 Madison Street
Tulsa, Oklahoma 74116
October 10, 2007

Dear Mr. Krohn:

Ron Bryden, class of 1967 here, coming at you out of the blue.

I haven't had anything to do with the Leverett School since the spring of 1969. At the time I was dead certain I'd never want to ever hear the name again, let alone be in touch.

Lately, though, I've been thinking that the time has maybe come to try and turn that around, with a few amends made. I'm hoping you'll agree.

*I saw on the news the other week that the bishop of
Kansas City is going to jail for having shielded abusive
priests in his diocese. And that the church is paying out
substantial settlements to the victims.*

*I wonder if you're aware of a not-so-dissimilar
situation at your own institution involving one of
your star pedagogues, the ones you're always touting as
embodying what makes a Leverett education so unique.
Imagine, faculty malfeasance at the Leverett School, of
all places! And with dire and enduring consequences for
yours truly.*

*I'm curious as to how this news strikes you, and
what you think should be done about it.*

I look forward to hearing from you very, very soon.

Most sincerely,

Ronald E. Bryden, Esq.

"He sounds a bit unhinged," Sam said.

"Or hurt and confused."

"And angry."

"You think?"

"And quite possibly litigious," Sam said. "Have you
responded?"

"Not yet, but I will. Sam, I need you to find out everything you can about Ron Bryden's career at Leverett. His academic record, who his teachers were, where he lived, why he left. Get me everything you can. On the q.t., please."

Boris gave Sam his trademark soulful stare. "We need Ron to understand how concerned we are, above all, about him," he added.

Really, there was no one like Boris.

"Suppose old Ron turns out to be a grifter?"

"We'll cross that bridge when we come to it. Right now, as far as we're concerned, he's a valued, long-lost member of the Leverett family with something potentially important to teach us.

"How are *you* doing, by the way?" he asked.

"Bearing up," Sam said, as noncommittally as possible. "Thanks for asking," he added, though Boris was the last person he wanted to discuss his marital situation with.

"Well, let me know if there's anything I can do."

"I appreciate that, chief." Sam rose stiffly, saluted, and made his exit.

HE WENT OUT AND SAT on the bench at the base of the Tower. At five-thirty this time of year the building lights were already blazing. If he squinted, the place looked like an ocean liner making its stately progress through the gathering dark. There was a veil across the half-moon. The air was as crisp as a Jonamac. The first frost had been forecast for tonight.

It all came back like the slap in the face of an unexpected wave. Of course he'd known Ron Bryden, though he hadn't crossed Sam's mind in forty years. He'd been Eddie's roommate. None of them could stand him.

FEBRUARY
1964

Pipe down, gentlemen. Let's get serious. For a change."

English 1, nearing the end of second term. Theodore Gibson, the most inventive, demanding, popular teacher in the school, was standing at the blackboard behind his desk. He had a smirk on his face—you might have thought it was a sneer if you didn't understand that it masked concern. He'd hung his olive-green corduroy jacket on the back of his chair and his white Oxford cloth shirt was rolled up to the elbows, with the top button undone, which meant that his striped knit tie was askew. He stared at the class, arms akimbo, through the tortoiseshell glasses that were always sliding down his shiny nose.

Mr. Gibson's room was on the second floor of Patterson, the humanities classroom building on the northeast rim of the Oval. In the blinding sun the sugar maples that lined School Street cast skeletal blue shadows on the snow, which was still miraculously white after two weeks of unbroken cold. It was getting toward the end of winter term and they were becoming next-to-impossible to control. They should have been outside having a schoolwide snowball fight or running on the shoveled paths from the gym to their dorms while their wet hair froze. Instead, they were cooped up inside, raring to make trouble.

The assignment had been to write a self-portrait, which was more than a bit daunting, given the animals in the class. Sam was cramped with anxiety, tense for battle. They all were.

"Darman, let's start with you."

Dave Darman, a rich kid from Houston, loved flaunting his superiority over the rest of them. He curled his pouty lower lip as he slouched at his desk in the third row, tossing his chestnut curls for additional effect. He read a snot-nosed little piece set in Rome, where his mother lived. Our hero meets raven-haired Ilaria in Piazza Navona and she invites him back to her parents' conveniently empty apartment with a view of Castel Gandolfo. Dot-dot-dot.

Several of the class applauded politely when he'd finished.

"I'll be in Rome over spring break," came a voice from the front row. "Can I have her number?"

"Right, she's so believable," muttered Ray Kaiser, who was sitting next to Sam in the back row. Ray was Sam's one friend at Leverett and they tended to see things—including Dave Darman—similarly.

Mr. Gibson merely nodded. "Sobiloff," he asked the boy to Darman's right, "what do you have to say for yourself?"

Sobiloff was a quiet day boy from West Hartford. His vignette, about helping out in his father's pharmacy and watching one of the clerks cheat a customer, was greeted with silence—the most devastating response of all.

"What's cooking, Brandt?" Gibson was pacing the room, fierce and imperious, as if he didn't know any of them from Adam.

Sam bent over his notebook and started reading a poem about his grandmother's death the previous summer. Hers had been his first death, really, and this was his first poem. In it he had everyone in the family say something about her, and after each of their quotes he'd written: *I miss you most.*

After he'd finished, Kaiser patted his shoulder consolingly. Again, no one said a thing.

At the bottom of the page Sam had drawn a drooping handkerchief in blue crayon. Gibson, looking over his shoulder, asked, "What's this, a crying towel?" Then, as he strode to his desk, he said to the class, "Let's talk about the poem's polyphony. The fact that it's written in different voices. What's the word, Kaiser?"

"He certainly seems to have loved his grandmother," Ray responded. His comment was either sympathetic or deeply cutting—Sam wasn't sure which.

"I'll say. What about you, Darman?"

"They all sounded pretty much the same to me," Dave said sourly, examining his nails.

"I'd like to see you try it. In fact, why don't we all do just that for next week's assignment? Write a theme in four different voices. Five pages."

The class groaned as Gibson dismissed them.

Sobiloff stopped Sam in the hallway. "That was really moving," he said gently. Sam hardly knew Jim, but he welled up as he thanked him.

IN SEPTEMBER his mother had sat weeping in their old Chevy station wagon as he walked up the path to Hollister House, the ivy-covered yellow-brick dormitory where he'd be living with fifty-nine other boys for the next four years. Earlier, his father had helped him haul his battered old trunk, which had been his when he'd gone off to Barton thirty years before, up to Sam's second-floor double. The trunk was neatly packed with his clothes, which had name tags sewn into every sweater and sock and pair of underwear. His father had insisted on sewn as opposed to iron-on tags, the effect no doubt of some trauma from his own school days—some remembered cruelty inflicted on him or someone else thanks to the inferior quality of his name tags. So Sam's mother had spent the summer sewing them into every piece of clothing he owned. They were beautiful things: SAMUEL C. BRANDT, JR. stitched in bright red sans-serif capitals on white silk ribbon—far more elegant than the button-down wash-and-wear shirts and chinos and Fruit of the Loom briefs they identified as his.

After his parents drove off he wandered around, staving off the inevitable. The school consisted of a group of ornate yellow-brick Gothic buildings with gabled roofs, once slate, now asphalt-tiled, and tall, thick agglomerations of chimneys—Victorian monstrosities, his mother called them, utterly unlike the neoclassical red-brick or stone complexes he'd seen at the other schools he'd applied to. There's little on the Leverett campus, in fact, to indicate the school's venerable age. The first two schoolhouses had burned down, and there hadn't been dormitories until well into the nineteenth century, as the boys had boarded with families in town. Which meant there was a remarkable uniformity to the look of the place, before the advent of mid-twentieth-century brutalism, that is, with the notable exception of the Georgian tower in the middle of the Oval. The school buildings fanned out on both sides of Main Hall or were dotted on the long slope that descended north to the meandering Leverett River, with its paired stone bridges, East and West, leading to the playing fields and the out-of-sight, deceptively tranquil but uncrossable Wachusett which the Leverett flowed into half a mile to the northeast. In spite of its architecture the place had presence: a modest, time-worn majesty.

He finally screwed up his courage and headed back to the dorm and down the hallway, funky with the freshly applied polish that made the green-and-yellow checkerboard linoleum floor gleam, varnished hairs, cookie crumbs, and all, then up the narrow oak-paneled staircase with its curved brass railing to meet his roommate, the still faceless, terrifying Hoagie Langhorne.

Hoagie turned out to be a lanky, big-eared, crew-cutted football player from an athletic family with a spiderweb of Leverett connections who took one look at Sam and decided he'd gotten a raw deal in the roommate sweepstakes. Sam soon learned that Hoagie enjoyed sauntering around their room in nothing but a madras jockstrap with the school's name emblazoned in gold block letters on the waistband. His contempt for Sam, though silent, was radioactive. Sam dressed in the closet.

The stronger boys' favorite entertainment apart from athletics was tormenting the weaker ones: shouting insults from the windows, body-checking them on the paths, short-sheeting their beds, shaming them in the locker rooms. With his pink glasses, green sneakers, and bowl haircut, Sam was an easy mark from the outset. Someone in the dorm called out "Eek!" when he came into the dining room one morning and for the rest of his time at Leverett he was known to one and all as Eek.

He was so homesick for his mother's cooking that he threw up every morning after breakfast, and was having trouble getting his bearings in French and math. Since he was still small—he hadn't yet turned fourteen—he'd been recruited as a cox. He'd seen pictures of his father's Barton

crew lined up brandishing their oars on the dock at Lake Tit-
icus, with their Abercrombie haircuts and dark shirts with
appliquéd white B's and tight chamois shorts arrestingly
filled out at the crotch. His father, no doubt, enjoyed the
idea of Sam reenacting yet another exploit from his own boy-
hood, one that would finally make a man out of him, though
nothing had worked so far. He was playing clarinet in the
band and defending right-wing positions in the debate club
for similar reasons. But he absolutely hated crew.

Rushes grew in thick clumps along the banks of the Leverett where the crew practiced and a noxious stink wafted
down from the paper mill several miles upstream. There
were rocks in the water, too, and the coach warned the coxes
to avoid the spots where they lurked beneath the surface.
Sam changed his boat's course far too often because he was
terrified of puncturing his fragile shell and intimidated by
the red-faced bigger boys facing him, pulling erratically on
their oars, which meant that instead of gliding evenly they
lurched forward by violent fits and starts, bouncing on the
water's hard surface while the coach in the motor launch behind them shouted exasperated instructions Sam couldn't
hear into his megaphone.

One dark, sodden afternoon, worn out and heartsick
after having only just managed to keep his boat from cap-
sizing in the rain, he was trying to dress unnoticed among
the steaming white bodies that crowded the locker room.

He was astounded by the display some of the boys made of themselves, parading in the aisles, slapping their towels, shaking their equipment, taunting each other.

Suddenly, a boy with a dark cowlick and glasses was saying, "So they have dicks. Guess what? We do, too. Or I do, anyway." The boy's head bobbed forward on his thin neck and his protuberant eyes homed in on Sam from behind thick black frames. His oily skin was erupting, like everyone else's only more so. His hair was plastered to his head and his shoulders were permanently hunched. He wore unacceptable white socks with unacceptable black loafers yet managed to exude an aura of arch superiority. Why was he talking to Sam?

Before long, though, he and Ray—for that was his name, Raymond Kaiser—were having extended exchanges, some conversational, some argumentative, day in and day out. Which meant, Sam figured, that by Leverett standards they had become friends—if you could call the clinging together of two despised loners friendship. But Sam was desperate for someone, almost anyone, to talk to. And so, it seemed, was Ray.

Soon they were more or less inseparable, at least when Kaiser made it clear, which wasn't always, that he wanted Sam around. Ray roomed in Boughton House, beyond the western edge of the Oval, in what was known as Siberia. With his mustard-colored India-print bedspread and wall hanging, his rubber plant in its lime-green pot, his enor-mous state-of-the-art stereo system, and the tape recorder on which he played language lessons in his sleep, Kaiser's digs were a far cry from the monastic cells of Sam and most of the other boys: bed, dresser, desk, and wooden school armchair, with maybe a pennant taped to the pea-green wall for decoration.

In November they sat together in the Boughton House common room, numb like everyone else, and watched Jack Ruby knock off Lee Harvey Oswald on live television.

Everything about Kaiser was foreign to Sam—intimidating, repellent, exciting. His father was a Phoenix lawyer who had worked for Barry Goldwater, though he didn't share the senator's reactionary politics the way Sam's father did. Sam eventually got a look at Walter Kaiser at grad-uation (Ray was too embarrassed—by Sam, or his own fa-ther, or both of them—to introduce them). A heavy-set man with combed-back white hair dressed in a black silk suit, white shirt, black tie, black Italian loafers, and black glasses like his son's, he was exotic compared to most of the Leverett fathers, Sam's included, in their cordovan bluchers and J. Press suits, with maybe a madras bow tie for a bit of prepster dash. Kaiser's father was both Western and Jewish, though his mother, Ray had been quick to let on, came from an old Arizona rancher family, whatever that meant. Sam had been vaguely aware of Jews at home—lawyer colleagues of his father's, their doctors, the family vet; but the notion that someone could be *half* Jewish was intriguing to someone like Sam desperately looking for advantages in being different.

Kaiser's mother and father, in his telling, came across as willful, indulgent, and hysterical—both hovering and absent. He seemed to despise them, though he shared their extravagant materialism. "Her decorator's a fag," Ray let drop about his mother one day. "He fell in love with me. She had a fit, but she couldn't give him up. So here I am."

Ray in turn denigrated Sam's parents' self-denying ways. Sam invited him to join them for dinner on one of their joyless visits. In his mind it was always brown weather as they trudged across campus to sports events he would never have dreamed of attending on his own; he tried to dodge other students and their families approaching on the paths while his mother dragged or was dragged by her slobbering Newfoundland and his father walked ahead, preoccupied and impatient, puffing furiously on the pipe clamped in his jaw.

They took Kaiser to a huge steakhouse in the next town, the kind of place that seats several hundred. Without asking, he ordered sour cream on his baked potato, which cost an extra quarter—an unheard-of extravagance in Sam's penny-pinching family. His father was incensed and let it show. Sam was mortified, by both of them.

After they left, Kaiser attacked their dowdiness and puritanism and Sam's lack of sophistication. "What do you know about food, or politics, or art, or anything? You're a rube, Brandt. Your parents are unbelievable. You haven't even heard of Freud. You need an education."

AND SO HIS EDUCATION BEGAN. Forget English, French, and Latin, where he was still just barely holding his own. Forget math, where he'd been assigned the dim-bulb hockey coach as his teacher. Sam became Kaiser's half-willing, horrified, and fascinated pupil as Ray exposed him to affluence, liberal politics, psychoanalysis, auto-suggestion, classical music, and sexual perversion. By spring he was writing home to report that he was reading Edward Albee's evisceration of marriage, *Who's Afraid of Virginia Woolf?*, for fun. His brother Alex, who would join him at Leverett the following year, complained that Sam had ignited their father's easily combustible wrath at the dinner table by asserting in his weekly letter home that he was old enough to read whatever he wanted.

His politics changed, too. Though Kaiser had only been at Leverett a couple of months, he'd already made friends with the school radical, a self-described antinuclear peacenik Commie fag named Malcolm Hurley. Hurley was the son of a federal bureaucrat. His open homosexuality had gotten mixed up in the minds of the masters, and maybe his mind too, with his protesting in support of the nascent civil rights movement. He was brilliant and shrill, a self-advertising, card-carrying pariah. (A few years later, in his airless, tentlike room at Harvard, he showed Sam a brilliant paper that argued for the homosexuality of Jesus and his disciples.)

What Malcolm enjoyed most was being subversive. Sam and Ray would sit in his room with Rich Mobley, one of the few Black kids in the school, and listen to Baez and Dylan and Odetta records, after which Malcolm and Rich and Ray would walk downtown to demonstrations that Sam didn't dare go near. Slowly, though, he came to see that his parents' ideas need not be his own. He learned to despise his father's reactionary views and relished saying so. Hanging around home during vacations, bored and lonely, he became an insufferably superior malcontent. His parents began to think that something had infected him, that sending him away to school had been a bad idea.

THEY WERE A TEAM: Ray was the captain and Sam the water boy. Only later did it occur to him that Kaiser had likely been as lonely as he was. The sullen, pretty roommate he'd been assigned, his own Hoagie Langhorne, didn't even bother to stop jerking off when Kaiser came into their room. He and Sam were oddball outcasts, partners in apartness. It was only later on that the pain of exclusion would metastasize into a shared sense of superiority over the stolid jockocracy.

There were a few other kids Sam tried making friends with. He went canoeing on the Leverett one autumn Sunday afternoon with a sour-faced boy from Texas named Ron Bryden, but they tipped over and had to walk home drenched and cold, and that was that. He got to know a few others in class he had nothing in common with or who were even more pathetic than he was. There was a strict economy to relationships at Leverett: you couldn't make friends down. That way lay utter ostracism.

In the spring he started spending time with Eddie Braddock, another knob in Hollister, and before long his world changed for good. Eddie and Ray became the poles of his existence at Leverett. Eddie would own him, body and soul. But it was Ray who had lifted Sam out of family servitude and set him on the excruciating path to self-creation—more than any of his teachers even, except perhaps for the mercurial Theo Gibson. Because of Ray, he hadn't been entirely alone.

In January Sam and Hoagie got free of each other and Sam moved to a single on the top floor of Hollister. Eddie's room was down the hall. Slowly, tentatively, they got familiar with each other—chatting in the hallway, eating in the dining room, doing homework. Suddenly, they were a kind of pair. Sam developed a terrible crush on him.

Edward Bridgman Braddock III was a slight, dark, agile boy from Seattle with a shock of black hair falling into his face over wire-rim glasses. His grandfather and namesake had made a fortune in grain and had gone on to be a five-term Republican senator from Washington, a sparring partner and rival of William O. Douglas, and an across-the-aisle mentor to Scoop Jackson.

Eddie was a long-distance runner and an obsessive biker. He kept an Italian racer in his room which he took out for long rides up and down the road along the Wachusett on Sunday afternoons. He loved Muddy Waters and played blues harmonica with an intensity that made some of the faculty wives uncomfortable enough to mention it. He often rode the edge of irritation and was quick to anger. He hated Leverett and made no effort to conceal it from his fellow students and the faculty. Sam was mesmerized by this dazzling, combustible kid. Before long he found he wanted much more in the way of closeness: to be near him, to watch him, to listen to him, and more than anything, to touch him.

One evening they were reading together on Eddie's bed. One of them shoved the other, the other shoved back, and before long they were wrestling. "I can beat you with my little finger, Brandt," Eddie snorted, pinning him effortlessly after the briefest of struggles. Sam kept pretending to fight but even then he understood that under Eddie, absorbing his heat, his breath, his scent, was where he wanted to be.

When there was a track meet, Sam would go watch him run. The first time, when Eddie saw him looking down from the upper level of the cage, the size of his surprised smile was an incredible reward, even if he ignored Sam for the rest of the race. If he was running longer distances, though, Sam could only make him out far off as he loped over the hump of East Bridge and across the playing fields, reappearing an hour later to hurl himself red-faced over the finish line. He was unreachable then, encased in pain and triumph or defeat.

One day while he was off on one of his thirty- or forty-mile rides, Sam stole into his room, which was always dark because he kept the curtains drawn. There was a bike wheel propped against the wall, his stereo, his recliner with a pole lamp beside it. A pair of tan corduroy Levi's lay on the linoleum floor in front of the Barcalounger, shucked in haste or fatigue.

The dorm was nearly empty, but Sam didn't dare close the door. He wanted desperately to take off his own pants and put Eddie's on. He felt magnetically drawn to them, knew they would invest him with a power he lacked. He picked them up and buried his face in their dirty creases, inhaling their holy funk. But everything in the room smelled of him—of Vitalis and Right Guard and his warm, light sweat overlaid by the lemon soap he loved. The Levi's' power and softness were intoxicating, but he was too afraid to put them on and he snuck out of the room ashamed.

Eventually Eddie was turned off by Sam's hovering adoration, and became tetchy and distant. Sophomore year he left Hollister and went to live in Urquhart, over by West Bridge, with Ron Bryden, one of his cross-country teammates. Sam would run into him on the stairs between classes or at the Grill and exchange stiff, proud greetings. Those were hard, long, hopeless months, yet they did nothing to alter his love for Eddie; if anything, they intensified it. He knew beyond a doubt that this love was the only thing that mattered, the best thing in him. The idea that he might find another friend never occurred to him. There was no one else.

His sophomore English teacher asked him to stay after class one day to discuss one of his themes. It was a portrait of a runner, a maladroit attempt to make sense of what had possessed him. Mr. Peters, a kindly, bespectacled man in his sixties, sat at his desk and tried delicately to caution the silent hothead hunched over his desk beside him about the difficulties of feelings neither of them could put a name to. But Sam had no interest in advice. What he wanted was more of the love he had dived into and was submerged in.

And then one frigid, starry December night, suddenly, miraculously, Eddie reappeared. After a glee club concert, they somehow found themselves standing together under the gate at the east side of the Oval pledging faith in one another. "I need you, Brandt," was all Eddie said. Sam had no idea how or why it had happened, but it was enough. For the rest of their time at Leverett they were inseparable.

Still, the anxiety that Sam's attachment to Ed was infected by sex always hung over them. Sam was miserable at home with nothing to do all summer. He played the cast-off records Eddie had given him, sent adoring letters to Seattle, where Eddie was with his girlfriend, the legendary Sally, and waited desperately, moony and sentimental, for Eddie's intermittent replies, penned in purple ink.

Sam tried to talk to his father about him once. They were sitting in the living room after dinner and Sam started talking about school and his great friend Eddie. "I suppose it's a kind of love," he ventured, proud that he'd found a way to give voice to his feelings and hungry for some kind of affirmation. His father coughed, lifted the newspaper off his lap to cover his face, and went back to his reading. After a while Sam said good night and went up to his room. It was the end of their relationship, in a way.

Sam replayed this scene again and again over the years, wondering whether his confession had uncovered buried feelings within his father. Like many men of his generation, he had no friends, really, but there were a few men he mentioned feelingly, old school chums who were no longer part of his life, a sad-sack client whose string of troubles seemed to arouse his sympathy. Was it possible his father had felt "a kind of love" for one of them? Or had Sam simply embarrassed him by calling attention to his own unmanly nature, by saying the unsayable? "Sammy's queer," his father told Alex once, with a little laugh, years later, when the three of them were kidding around one afternoon. That was all he ever had to say on the subject.

The minute Sam got back from vacation he'd make a beeline for Eddie's room and hold him as long and as tightly as he'd allow. Eddie would return Sam's embrace at first, then gently push him away. "My father read your letters," he told Sam during one of these reunions. "He says you're queer and I should stay away from you." Another enemy father, something else they shared—though when Sam finally met

Mr. Braddock, a tall, courtly, morose man, at graduation, he found he was deeply drawn to him.

"What did you tell him?" Sam asked hotly, darkly.

"I told him it wasn't like that. But sometimes I worry that your feelings for me are . . ."

"Are what?"

"You know, sexual."

"They're not, Eddie. It's another kind of love."

Just what kind of love theirs was, though, was never sorted out by either of them. Sam was desperate for Eddie's touch, yet he was determined, too, that the nobility of their bond not be tainted by neurosis. But everything he did at Leverett was filtered through his vassallike devotion. He ate his meals with or without Eddie, always knowing where he was, and they spent every evening till curfew together in his room. When they were in sync, Sam was happy, grounded, productive. If there was trouble between them, he was distracted and listless. He worked; he excelled in his studies and eventually earned his way from the outer rim of alienation to what felt like a grudging meritocratic acceptance. With Kaiser and Darman, he became one of the intellectual capos of the class. But the most important thing in Sam's life, day in and day out, his love for Eddie, was something that went unspoken, except between themselves.

Once they were going somewhere, to a movie or the Grill. It had turned chilly and Ed unthinkingly handed Sam a sweater. He had no idea of the gift he was giving; if he had, he might have withheld it. Wearing his sweater, Sam was advertising himself as his, walking radioactive beside him in his wine-red crewneck. When he surrendered it reluctantly before going home some of its protective warmth and magic stayed with him.

He was dismayed by the skeletal, neurasthenic creature he saw in the mirror. Who could love him? Certainly he did not feel lovable. What he felt was an irresistible tropism toward Eddie's knotted masculine integrity, his warmth, his litheness, which he could only experience in those tight embraces that both did and didn't express his attraction and longing for tenderness. Eddie was the actor, the heroic loner, the fearless outlier always on the verge of rebellion, just out of reach: not openly in need of adoration, never acknowledging that Sam might be as essential to him as he was to Sam, yet somehow frank, too, in his loyalty and attachment. And maybe Sam needed him that way: to keep him at bay, to hold off the desired but impossible, feared explosion that would undo his tenuous grip on their little world.

There were other pairings-off among the boys which were likely as virginal as theirs, and everyone was aware and respectful of them. There were roommate marriages: Boitani and Ragen were a pair all the way through school and college, often spending the evening sitting in their room with the lights out. There were actual flesh-and-blood love affairs, too, Sam learned later: Stearns, a pock-faced, hyper-intense kid in Sam's year, told him after graduation that he'd had a long and blissful secret relationship with Muschamp, tall and handsome if something of a mama's boy, all through their four years.

A few students openly (or covertly) called themselves homos, or queers as they put it; once in a while they were found out and made to withdraw. Malcolm Hurley told Sam many years later that he and his roommate, who'd been sur-prised in bed by a teacher, had to undergo psychiatric "cures" which led, he claimed, to his friend's eventual suicide. Now and then, too, a teacher made an unwanted approach to a student; soon it was announced that he had moved on to another school. In this all-male community, with only the faculty wives and daughters and an occasional girl from the town for leavening, love among the boys was tacitly acknowl-edged and rigorously guarded against.

Mostly, there was boasting about girls at home, or about alcohol-fueled sex with a mother's friend or a friend's mother. Eddie told Sam his own mother's best friend had seduced him at a drunken barbeque on Mercer Island and wanted to keep seeing him—but he was loyal to Sally. "My own small pleasure is so insignificant compared to hers," he said, a little sanctimoniously, Sam thought. Eddie seemed to pity Mrs. Halstead her loneliness, her desperate need to be touched. Sam didn't know how to ask him what had happened, having nothing to offer in return, though he had his own unspoken crush that summer on his mother's best friend, with her wide, dark features and maternal gentleness, so different from his everyday matter-of-fact mother.

Most of the boys were as inexperienced as he was, and just as desperate to conceal it. When the girls were bused in from Miss Porter's or Westover for that barbaric form of intramural athletics known as the dorm dance and the catcall "Tuna!" echoed across the Oval, nearly all of them, Sam included, went in for the sweaty clinch on the basketball court followed up with anxious professions of love in letters that usually went unanswered. Which went to prove what foreign creatures girls were, though most of them had sisters.

No one entered their closed circle. Each of them had his own friends. Sam had Kaiser and, at times, the terrifying Dave Darman and a few others. Eddie barely acknowledged their existence. This crowd was mainly his fellow runners, including the studly Johnny Pratt. But his and Sam's togetherness was separate from these connections. It was a thing apart.

GIBSON ENCOURAGED THE BOYS' inner delving more creatively than any of the other teachers. "What's up, Brandt?" he'd ask, all of a sudden. "Has a radical notion maybe entered your fumbled head?" His classes were free-form, willfully chaotic. He had the kids lead sessions, made them role-play, write skits about each other, and perform them for the group. They critiqued his own writing, too. He'd published some opaque essay-poem-stories in little magazines which he had them discuss and imitate, encouraging them to be ruthless in their criticism (they loved it). He showed them that writing was a dynamic activity, not something ossified on the page but an open, ever-changing avenue of communication between one person and another. He was more an impresario than a dispenser of information—though he was an unbending stickler for grammar. As the adviser to Drama Club, he directed their winter and spring productions—Beckett, Albee, Pinter, Wilder, Ben Jonson, and Shakespeare—which were the high point of the year for the aesthetes.

Gibson didn't fraternize with the boys, though he sometimes came close. He was one of those adults who wanted it understood that he was on the side of Youth: free-thinking, unconventional, one of them, really; not a stodgy, hidebound oldster. The other masters eyed him with scornful fascination. Gibson was certainly not one of *them* as far as they were concerned, though he was a crack teacher and a passable coach, even if he was a heavy smoker. For them, as for the boys, he was an unsettling class A eccentric.

He seemed to have touched down in central Connecticut from the moon. Theo had already been at Leverett for seven or eight years by the time Sam had him in class, which meant he was in his mid-thirties, verging on old age. He was tall and wiry, if far from athletic—and single, which was out of the ordinary for the masters in his cohort, though there was a cadre of confirmed bachelors among the older generation. He never mentioned his family, but it was thought that he went home to visit his mother in Worcester on weekends.

There was a rumor he was illegitimate, that his father was the ne'er-do-well son of a decayed New Orleans family who'd traveled north, knocked up a girl, and vanished back where he came from. Some detected a slight Southern lilt in Gibson's accent, especially when he'd had a drink or two. On his mother's side he was reputedly of Greek extraction, as his leathery skin and thick dark hair, combed back in a duck-tail, seemed to confirm. In contrast with his buttoned-down peers in their tweed jackets and chinos, Gibson wore Levi's like the boys, un-ironed shirts, invariably white, and scuffed bluchers or Hush Puppies. Today you might call him a hipster.

Theo told Sam, in one of his rare self-revealing moments, that he'd been a classics major who'd minored in English at Columbia. He'd decided to teach for a while instead of going straight on to graduate school, and the only attractive opening had been in the Leverett English department; he'd given it a go and was still here a decade later. He coached j.v. track and cross-country—Eddie, who disdained and ignored most of the coaches, rated him highly and usually took his advice. He smoked nonstop while he watched the boys run their sprints and hurdles. Smoking was still tolerated at Leverett in those days. There were butt rooms in the dorm basements where the most disaffected of the kids, the negos, gathered to bitch and plot revenge. But Gibson was an extreme smoker, a three-pack-a-day man. His clothes, his apartment, his skin were suffused with nicotine. The kids called him Smokehouse when they were feeling derisive or fearful, and Theo when they adored him, which was far more often.

He could be flirtatious in class in an acid kind of way, especially with the athletes. He made fun of their tongue-tied malapropisms, their inarticulate complacency, their readiness to fold at the slightest intellectual challenge, with a kind of amorous disdain that was a joy to witness. *You think the world revolves around you, you dumb lugs, as in fact it does, unfairly and ridiculously, and it's unfair and ridiculous but nevertheless delightful that I can't help being charmed by you myself,* he seemed to be saying, with a shake of the head and a grin that included himself in his doing-down of human folly. It was clear that Theo had a sort of a thing for a tongue-tied, pie-faced football player in his 4B who was thick in more ways than one. The kid blushed bright red to be the butt of Gibson's loverly contempt in the classroom, though he would have reacted violently if anyone had dared to allude to the game he and Theo were playing. Everyone, including the kid, was in on the good, harmless, if not quite clean fun, and they joked about it among themselves. It was part and parcel of the Gibson mystique. Somehow it only made him cooler.

Sam couldn't have been more unlike Theo's denigrated and cherished athletes, but now and then he'd be invited to performances or exhibitions in Hartford—*Messiah*, a chamber group, a Whistler show at the Atheneum. It was only later on that he came to see how he'd benefited from Gibson's paternal interest, what a void it had filled in his timorous adolescence. Slowly, Gibson became Sam's sounding board and source of wisdom. Once, he'd been complaining about the pressure he felt from his father to go to law school and eventually work with him in his suburban office south of Boston. Theo looked down his shiny nose at him and said, "You're not going to be a lawyer, Sam. You have other things to do in life." Sam had no idea what Theo imagined he might be: a librarian, perhaps, or an English teacher, like him. Once he'd said it, though, a weight Sam hadn't known had been sitting on him almost immediately lifted and before long he told his father he wasn't going to be a lawyer.

By third year who they were going to be, more or less—who they'd always been, maybe, and who they were to each other—had started to come clear. They were becoming themselves.

It was obvious to everyone that Theo's favorite, the one he was most fully in sync with, was Darman. Dave, in his Weimaraner-colored chamois blazer, with his luxuriant stream of put-downs, was the class show-off, triumphantly confident, insolent, self-possessed, the coolest of the cool.

If Kaiser was intellect for Sam, and Eddie pure heroic masculinity, Darman embodied a lowering, feline knowing-ness. He slouched like an upper-middle-class James Dean, offering a running commentary out of the side of his mouth. He loved shocking the masters as well as his fellow students, and his being more gloriously, gluttonously bourgeois than the rest of them was key to his power. His androgynous pout was matched by his luxuriant wardrobe: twenty jackets to everyone else's two or three, leather and cashmere to their corduroy and gabardine. Suede was Darman's substantial essence. Sam would covet his chamois jacket all his life.

Darman's father, a former major league ballplayer, had been divorced by his oil heiress mother for his philandering ways. The afterimage of Herb Darman's career as a third baseman for the Royals was the only thing athletic about his son. Far more arresting was his aura of polymorphous carnal sophistication. Nothing was news to Darman: not just the everyday facts of life that obsessed them all, but worlds of unimaginable sybaritic damnation beyond. He had large brown eyes whose hound-dog bedroom dreaminess was enhanced by the bluish tinge of the bags beneath them. Maybe Darman wasn't getting enough sleep for all the right reasons. Or maybe he was unhappy like the rest of them—only lonelier, more wracked by lust. There was no way to penetrate his facade, though Sam had garnered an inkling of his essential nature in the locker room when he noticed how much darker his pendulous cock was than the rest of his body. David Darman was mad, bad, and dangerous to know.

When Dave was at his most preening Sam would notice Gibson observing him with a Cheshire cat smile, enjoying his humiliation of his victims. Gibson recruited him to Drama Club—not that he really had to try, since it was where the sophisticated kids in the school naturally gravitated. And Dave was the star of every one of Gibson's productions, whether it was *Waiting for Godot*, in which he was a febrile Vladimir opposite Johnny Pratt's laconic Estragon; or Volpone in Ben Johnson's eponymous worldly-wise satire of greed and self-dealing; or the cross-dressing lead in Io-nesco's *The Bald Soprano*. No one had a legitimate reason to complain, though, because Darman was hands down the most exhibitionist and histrionic of all of them. Sam loved watching Theo move him around the stage like a prop, ad-justing his stance and the jut of his chin. Dave always took Gibson's tart direction in stride, working to fulfill and even anticipate his mentor's wishes. He aimed to please Theo in a way he never did with anyone else.

"A Genghis Kahn of the affections," Kaiser called Dar-man, and he knew better than anyone, for what Ray was to Sam—an intellectual authority, a psychic overlord—Darman was for Ray, though with a more sinister, absolutist edge, given that the two of them were playing for ultimate king-of-the-hill stakes. They were the class stars, miles ahead of everyone else, but Dave could reduce Ray to confusion and incoherence with a dismissive glance.

"Come off it, Kaiser," he'd sigh when Ray started spin-ning his analytic spiderwebs. "We've had enough of your ra-tiocination." And Kaiser, instead of barreling on the way he would have if Sam had had the temerity to complain, would turn tongue-tied, mumble an excuse, and wander off.

It was a matter of pride with Darman that he had no conscience, but Kaiser did, even if he liked to act otherwise. Whom did Dave open up to, who was the Dave to his Ray? No one, as far as Sam knew—unless it was Theo. Dave was the undisputed khan, the king of their hill who could pulverize the rest of them at will. There was something feral, reptilian, about Darman. You sensed that he took his pleasure where he found it, wolfing it down and slinking off to digest it in a corner alone.

Every now and then a fresh enthusiasm would attract his attention for a while, as happened with Eddie's friend Johnny after they'd starred in *Godot* together. Sam and the rest of them soon got tired of hearing how suave, how nonchalant, how ineffably cool Pratt was. They could see it for themselves: Pratt was the best-looking kid in the class, a superb athlete, even-tempered, loose-limbed, unflappable, and invariably kind to boot—he seemed thirty, not seventeen, meaning that he couldn't have cared less about the jockeying for dominance that preoccupied Dave, Ray, Sam, and the rest of them. Which no doubt was why Dave set his cap for him.

Dave took Johnny off to Rome to visit Dave's mother over Christmas that year. When they returned, there was no more talk about Johnny's superior attributes. Soon, it was another classmate, Oz Morton, whose parents owned a vineyard in Napa, who became the focus of Dave's interest.

There was always a pile of dirty Brooks Brothers shirts—yellow, blue, and pink, though never white—in a corner of Oz's room. Someone said he didn't bother having them washed but kept ordering new ones. He was short, with a gravelly voice, and his chin was always rough with golden stubble. He dressed for church in classic prep-elegant style: overcoat, dark suit, and penny loafers with actual pennies in the slots. Darman and he were inseparable that winter. Sam and Ray used to see Dave with Oz and a demure French girl he was courting, whose grandfather was reputedly a great international financier, in the art gallery on Saturday afternoons. She'd be driven over from Miss Porter's and they'd sit together, he in coat and tie, she in a cocktail dress, making polite conversation while Dave entertained them.

That spring vacation Eddie took the Transcontinental Express west, and Darman and Oz went along with him as far as Chicago. No one ever knew exactly what happened on the trip, but whatever it was, Eddie told Sam that the chumminess between Dave and Oz turned to ice overnight.

"All of a sudden Oz stopped talking," Eddie said. "He sat alone in the observation car and got off with no warning at Gary."

Whatever had happened, hatred bloomed between him and Darman. Oz went stony at the mere mention of his name.

Kaiser recognized an opportunity when he saw one. His weekly column in the *Hutch*, "The Trail of the Inchworm," was eagerly read across campus for its spikiness and snark. Few at Leverett, if you left out Darman and Theo, were a match for Ray's acid tongue, which meant he was feared and disliked, both by the faculty, who instinctively mistrusted him, and the other kids, who dreaded being the butt of his satire. He was constantly testing the rules and the boundaries of taste, which more than once got him in Dutch with the administration. He generally knew just how far to go, though, and the Head, Reginald Heber, clearly enjoyed his sass, even if he acted put out.

"He calls me up to his office to reprimand me, but before long he's asking me what I think about this issue and that," Ray boasted.

"I bet you love that," Sam said.

"Heber's a real operator. He reminds me of one of my father's partners. He's a political animal through and through."

Ray's column about the Darman-Oz debacle took the form of a twisted retelling of a famous old Edward Lear ballad. An owl and a pussycat go to sea in a beautiful pea-green boat. All is bliss until something terrible but unspecified happens, the boat gets upended, and the pussycat ends up with the mince, the quince, *and* the runcible spoon, while the owl is left to moan in a tree alone.

It was unclear who among Kaiser's readers knew the true import of his parable, but it was as plain as day who was the winner and who the loser in the transaction—especially with the cartoon, drawn by Sam, featuring the pussycat's luxuriant head of hair and the owl's stubbled chin. Darman, unsurprisingly, affected not to notice a thing. But Oz understood perfectly. He never spoke to Kaiser, or Sam, again.

RAY'S BEST FRIEND, apart from Sam, was Gideon Jonas, the mind-bogglingly brilliant son of a New York psychiatrist. Gideon was one of Kaiser's few intellectual equals and their repartee was like championship table tennis, hard to follow but glorious to witness. They spoke a language no one else could make sense of, given that fellatio, Oedipal jealousy, and anality were not common parlance at Leverett, at least in those days. Gideon loved to shock. One of his favorite moves was to quote his father, who claimed that a good shit was far more sensually satisfying than intercourse.

Sam loved the bons mots that dripped from Jonas's harelip. Being with him and Ray made him feel like a member of a society the rest of the world didn't know existed, or a visiting fireman anyway. But Gideon, who was a year ahead of them and who Sam later learned had started taking heroin, hanged himself one spring weekend of his freshman year at Yale.

It was inevitable that Darman would turn his sights on Eddie. Something about him drew Dave. Was it the patina of "normality" that masked his inner turmoil? Sam asked himself. Was it his grandfather's prominence, or that Dave knew he mattered to Sam? Whatever it was, Darman locked on and wouldn't let go. Worst of all, Eddie responded.

"What do you see in him?" Sam asked.

"Darman is cool," was all Eddie would say, annoyed by Sam's pettiness, no doubt. Of course Darman was cool. That was the problem.

That spring Gibson started taking the two of them down to New York for outings. A few of the hipper bachelor masters occasionally offered this kind of privilege. Sam affected to be too proud to notice, but he was a cauldron of envy.

One Sunday, after yet another of these jaunts, he couldn't help asking where they'd gone.

"To Yankee Stadium. For a doubleheader," Eddie shot back. "Now are you satisfied?"

Yankee Stadium! None of them was a baseball fan, but Darman, of course, knew the game inside out and he'd been terrific at explaining team strategy. They'd had a fabulous time. There was nothing Sam could say.

Finally, mysteriously, he was invited along. This time they were going to the Museum of Modern Art, in those days still a warren of knocked-together buildings on West Fifty-Third Street. It was Sam's dazzling first exposure to cubism and surrealism and Pollock and de Kooning and Picasso's *Guernica*, the unquestioned linchpin of the place; but Eddie and Darman, it turned out, both knew and loved MoMA, having gone there with their parents numerous times on visits to the city. Sam couldn't help being impressed by the way they ambled through the galleries discussing their favorite Mirós and Matisses while he had to content himself with a lecture from Theo about the glories of abstract expressionism.

Afterward they had a burger on Sixth Avenue before driving back. Theo kept the conversation alive, asking what they thought of what they'd seen. Darman was sitting up front with him, but he kept turning back to engage Ed.

"What was your favorite Picasso? Blue period, rose?"

"Maybe *Night Fishing at Antibes*. I loved the eerie light, the mystery."

Sam saw other sides of Eddie that day: not only his aliveness to art, but how he and Gibson enjoyed ganging up on Darman, who became sober, anxious, it seemed, about the impression he was making in a way he never would have with

Kaiser or Sam. In their little foursome stuffed into Gibson's Beetle, it was Gibson and Eddie who were the arbiters and enforcers of the day's lessons. Darman kept floating his own airy notions, but Eddie, who had no need to impress, stuck to his own ideas and Sam became aware not only of Darman's but of Theo's respect for him. He was proud of his friend, proud that his love was being vindicated. He reached over and held Eddie's hand while the others talked, half following their repartee, half listening to Neil Diamond wailing on the radio, overwhelmed by excitement and adoration in the lit-up dark.

There were a few of these outings. Then Theo announced he'd invited Ron Bryden, of all people, to join them. No one was thrilled, but there wasn't a lot they could do about it.

"Why Ron?" Sam asked Darman, almost whining.

"Theo says the kid feels left out when we take off without him," Darman told him.

"How does he even know?"

Dave shrugged. "Maybe Braddock brags about the great times we have."

"Has Ron been hinting that he wants to come along on outings with Theo?" Sam asked Eddie that evening while he was noodling on his harmonica.

"No way," he responded, his tone hovering as usual between deadpan and sardonic, its querulous timbre piercing Sam's heart as always. "I hardly talk to the guy, even if I'm well aware of how he looks butt-naked. And it ain't a pretty picture, I can tell you."

They knew they had to accept that Ron was coming along on their next adventure. Since Theo's VW was too small for five, he asked T. D. Tompkins, who sometimes co-directed Drama Club productions with him, to come along. Darman and Ron ended up driving down with Theo, while Eddie and Sam went with T.D. in his snazzy little Triumph convertible.

T.D., an overdressed, smooth-as-silk admissions officer in his late twenties, seemed like an odd sidekick for Theo. He appeared to have sailed under the administration's faulty gaydar, though the kids were on to who and what he was. "Go, go, T.D." they chanted behind his back whenever he sauntered by. Still, the passion he and Theo shared for dramatics had resulted in some memorable productions. They occasionally went on joint scouting trips to London, bringing back news about innovations in English theater which they did their best to put into practice at Drama Club. Their spectacular production of *Volpone* had featured Great White Hunter animal heads borrowed from the walls of Alumni Hall and paraded around the stage on poles by football players in loincloths and Egyptian headdresses and little else.

T.D. was an ingratiating chatterbox on the way down to the city, prying about their families and friends while revealing next to nothing about himself. "I cannot stand this guy," Eddie said under his breath when they made a pit stop for gas and a pee on the Merritt Parkway. Luckily, they'd be driving back with Theo.

They were going to a matinee performance of García Lorca's *Blood Wedding* staged by the Living Theatre at the Circle in the Square. Julian Beck and Judith Malina, as the play's illicit lovers, came down into the audience stark naked and hassled the spectators. It was meant to be shocking and threatening, and it was; but Ron was the most disturbed of all of them. "Aren't there laws against this?" he complained, going rigid in his seat as the actors approached. Theo said, "Relax, Ron. It won't kill you. I know this doesn't happen in Dallas. Which is why you're here."

The Living Theatre was their last New York boondoggle, as it turned out. Darman dropped hints about another outing or two with Theo and Bryden, and Gibson took Sam to hear Stravinsky's *Sacre du printemps* in Hartford at the end of the season. But Ron had been the party pooper. He, and T.D., had spoiled their fun.

Another boy a couple of years behind Sam told him years later that T.D. had tried to blackmail him into sleeping with him while he was in Tompkins's English 3 class. He'd heard, too, that T.D. liked to take Web Breeden, a willowy kid from Tucson, out for drives in the Triumph. One day he pulled over and told Web he was in love with him. Web asked to be driven back to his dorm and was.

Soon enough Tompkins was history. A few years later he reportedly got in trouble for having an affair with a student at Barton. Tompkins claimed the kid had seduced him—that he, in effect, was the victim. He moved on somewhere out West and was never heard from again.

DARMAN TOLD KAISER, who lost no time relaying the news to Sam, that he and Johnny had had a friendly lovemaking session on their trip to Rome. Dave described it as an act of camaraderie, a mutual experiment of no great importance to either of them. But Darman's third-year art project featured a nude snapshot of Pratt that felt reverential to Sam.

Kaiser lost no time making an approach to Johnny himself, but predictably got nowhere. As usual, he strained to be Dave's peer in lawlessness, but he couldn't pull it off.

That summer Ron left Leverett for good. No one knew why, least of all Eddie, who learned about it in a letter from his advisor. He swung into action and managed to secure Johnny as his roommate in Bryden's place. Sam hardly knew Johnny, but he was so self-possessed and unpetty that he couldn't help admiring him. Had he and Darman really slept together? Sam could imagine Johnny doing it just to get Darman off his back. What he couldn't do was imagine him caring.

Dave stayed at Leverett that summer, which seemed odd given how boring he was always complaining it was. He had a job in the admissions office showing prospective students around and helped Gibson produce the summer school plays in his spare time.

Ray rented an apartment in Cambridge, on a bleak stretch of Massachusetts Avenue north of Harvard Square. College was rearing its threatening head: they'd be applying in the fall. Leverett being a traditional feeder school for Harvard, in any given year about fifty of them would be picking up and moving to Cambridge after graduation; Kaiser was giving it an early try. He'd enrolled in the summer school, purportedly to study Russian. Sam couldn't imagine his parents allowing him this kind of freedom, but Ray took it as his due. It occurred to Sam, not for the first time, that maybe Ray wasn't all that welcome back in Phoenix. He took language classes in the Yard, smoked a lot of dope, and masturbated nonstop, he told Sam. Sam visited him a couple of times—anything to get away from the do-nothing boredom of home. They went to movies in the Square, haunted the bookstores and coffee houses, and sat around gossiping. Ray claimed that their classmate Orin Masterson and his sister Gwen, who lived on Brattle Street nearby, were both trying to get him into bed, but Sam had his doubts.

Eddie was out in Seattle with Sally, learning photography. Sam got one letter back for every three he wrote and thought he sensed a restlessness, an incipient melancholy in his friend, despite his endless crowing about how wonderful it was to be home. Sam hated being at home himself. He mowed the lawn, read books Kaiser recommended by Norman O. Brown and Herbert Marcuse that were way over his head, bickered with his brother, daydreamed about Eddie, and masturbated nonstop.

Late in August he had a visit from one of his neighbors in the dorm, a boy named Paul Buell whose nineteenth-century romance with a willowy, snobbish, neurasthenic kid from San Antonio Sam had witnessed firsthand. Paul was a wealthy boy from Boston, grand and grandmotherly, who liked to wrap himself in a Chesterfield with a huge fur collar and walk across campus on winter nights. There had been lots of carrying on and swooning about hurtful things the two either had or hadn't done to each other, operatic late-night scenes, tearful partings and reconciliations, and then a definitive break.

Now Paul drove down to Hingham to visit Sam. He brought lobsters and champagne in a hamper, which they lunched on in an empty corner of the town beach, ignoring the stares of the other bathers. As he was leaving, Paul handed Sam a copy of Thomas Mann's *Stories of Three Decades*. "Read 'Death in Venice,'" he advised solemnly. "It explains everything."

Sam was mystified by Buell's visit. He wondered later, as he consumed that bible of an aging man's obsession with an unreachable boy, what Paul knew about him that he didn't know himself. Had he come to initiate Sam into the neurasthenic brotherhood of unhappy men who loved other men? It didn't occur to Sam until much later that he might have been being vetted as a stand-in for Buell's abandoned friend.

DARMAN PLAYED HAMLET THAT FALL, under Gibson's direction, and he did it masterfully. His unselfconscious self-display made him the perfect avatar of eighteen-year-old disaffection.

Every class has its Hamlet: Lars Halbreich, later managing partner of Goldman, Sachs, was Hadley's that year; Andover had Eric Erlanger, who went on to be a major daytime soap star. Leverett's mascot of lusting teenage ambition and anxiety was David Darman. Sam could still remember him years later, holding Yorick's skull, the sensual torque with which he lifted it to eye level and how his girlish hips filled out his princely tights.

That was the night Gibson introduced Sam to Sandy Pleyel's father, the great Paul, who was in the audience. Sam at that point knew next to nothing about who he really was, except that he was a celebrated artist and the Most Important Person he had so far encountered, his first truly remarkable character. And he was wowed by Pleyel's warmth and congeniality with his son's friends.

Was it put on? Pleyel seemed so intensely interested in everything at Leverett, including them. He was like a grown-up version of his adorable son, who was playing Horatio to Dave's Hamlet. Sandy had arrived as a knob in Sam's third year, a beguiling sprite who shared his father's sanguine temperament and was utterly protected from reality by his unquestioning love. Having spent his young life being coddled by his celebrated father—his mother was seldom mentioned—Sandy seemed to take it for granted that everyone else loved him, too, and because he expected it, they tended to.

"We have a living room two stories tall lined with books from floor to ceiling overlooking the East River. And a box at the Met. I go every night. When you come for a visit, I'll take you." More than the luxury of Sandy's life, it was the way he took it for granted that astounded Sam; the great world of Manhattan from which his young friend sprang was as matter-of-fact to him as their everyday hometowns were to the rest of them.

Pleyel was arguably the most celebrated parent at Leverett, apart from the bankers and functionaries whose names sometimes showed up in the papers. Paul—he insisted they call him by his first name—was the youngest, the most accessible and worldliest, not to say the most successful, of the post–abstract expressionist generation, a kinder, gentler older cousin of Andy Warhol with an enormous studio downtown and galleries all over the world. It had reportedly been a shock to his New York friends when Paul had chosen to send his one child, Sandor, or Sandy, the absolute apple of his eye, away to Leverett.

Sam at seventeen had not yet reached his full height, which would turn out to be a very average five feet eleven, but he was already several inches taller than Sandy's father. He could see a tighter, more manicured version of his ragamuffin son in Paul's deeply tanned face, his swept-back salt-and-pepper hair and thin tortoiseshell frames. Sam would become familiar with his art only later, but he loved the miniature watercolors of every-day objects—books, keys, a bunched-up sweater—that Sandy tacked up on the wall in his room, and which Sam stared at evening after evening as they worked through the declensions of Latin nouns together. They were always his favorite Pleyels.

He'd offered to coach Sandy in Latin, a subject the younger boy had constant trouble with. Sam would show up after dinner a couple of nights a week and while Sandy pretended to bend to his books he'd stare at his surprisingly broad back in the mirror, smell the musk of his hair oil and the fetor of dried semen in the wadded-up Kleenex in his wastebasket, and go half-drowsy from the heat their bodies radiated in his little box of a room. At nine-fifteen he'd say good night and drop in on Eddie, who lived downstairs, before walking home.

Ray saw red whenever Pleyel was mentioned. "That man is an utter fraud," he'd mutter under his breath. "He has no talent whatsoever." Which was so patently untrue that Sam knew Kaiser was giving vent to other feelings. Sandy tended to gravitate to Darman and Sam, and to Dave in particular, so Sam simply assumed that Ray was jealous.

Sam picked up somewhere—or had he imagined it?—that Darman and Paul had a relationship at some point. Was it freshman year of college when he and Dave were rooming together? No wonder he was always in New York. Sam couldn't believe it could have gone on while they were still at Leverett—or had it? He wondered whether it was watching Dave declaim "To be or not to be" on that cramped little stage in the old Methodist church where Drama Club performed in those days that had gotten the great man's attention. But he and Dave were likely already acquainted, for Darman and Sandy had become buddies the instant Sandy arrived at Leverett. Maybe that was why Pleyel was there that weekend, in fact—to watch them both perform. When Sam first saw Pleyel's portrait of Darman propped casually on the mantel of his Cambridge apartment their senior year at Harvard—you can see it now for yourself at the Los Angeles County Museum of Art—his open-mouthed, chin-up grin, exaggerated by Paul's neo-expressionist palette, had shocked him: could this be the churlish boy he thought he knew?

But he shouldn't have been surprised. There were people, Eddie included, whom Dave Darman was eager to please. And in Paul Pleyel maybe he'd found someone he could look up to and even love.

KAISER MOVED INTO HOLLISTER for their senior year and was assigned a humble single on the first floor. Finally, he and Sam were housemates.

Ray's next-door neighbor, the hockey-playing son of an admiral who had a stiff crew cut and a buff body, paraded around the dorm in nothing but a towel talking tough like an apprentice Brando. Kaiser told Sam he kept trying to get Dee into bed, but never got anywhere with him.

Ray and Dee were also competing for the affections of Angie Ahern, the redheaded wife of the history master who lived in the third-floor apartment below Theo's with their three children. Kaiser claimed she encouraged his attentions; Sam had heard—not from him—that she made a pass at Dee, and did, Kaiser reported, go to bed with him twice. (Or maybe he made it up; Sam could never be quite sure. But Kaiser usually stopped short of pure fiction, and it wasn't like him to keep this kind of news a secret.)

That fall a famous poet came to Leverett for a couple of days, hosted by the English department, and the Aherns gave a party where a lot of drinking was done by the grown-ups. "Onward and inward, Angie," was how the great man toasted his hostess. For the rest of the year, "Onward and inward!" was their rallying cry.

Sam was a proctor senior year, which meant patrolling the halls at night, checking the other boys in, holding the volume down, keeping the peace. He loved the work because it gave him the chance to suss out what was going on in the dorm. You could tell a lot if you kept your eyes open: who was in, who was engaged, who was unhappy, who was up to no good.

The dorms were hotbeds of adolescent lust. There were no secrets:

Stone made love to his mattress several times a day. His dick got infected and he had to take antibiotics.

Herrick, a stunning Black kid from New York who was well over six feet tall, claimed he could suck himself off.

Haines, a goofy lug from Hawaii, told Sam he was a transvestite. He had an aquarium in his room and used strong-smelling acne medicine. He showed Sam his books about female impersonation, but Sam never got to see his dresses.

Lou Ross, a day boy, had a townie girlfriend he saw every afternoon. Eventually, he got her pregnant and there was a collection among the students to raise cash for an abortion—their first experience of organized charity. Lou didn't get kicked out the way Tim Doran did the next year for a similar offense, because no one on the faculty found out.

Sobiloff, as normal a kid as you could imagine—open, gentle, gawky, funny, sentimental—kept saying he wanted to fuck Donny Durbin, a cute-faced, rosy-cheeked little pixie who clearly also rang Mr. Dunand's bell. Sobiloff was so open and natural about his feelings that anyone who didn't admit to wanting to fuck Durbin—who was still young enough to be girlish, the best available female substitute— seemed twisted and repressed.

There was a lacrosse player on the second floor whose surly sensuality Sam found distracting. His admiration must have made itself felt, because Kaiser eventually told him to leave the kid alone.

On the fourth floor, across from Gibson's apartment, a square-jawed Argentine princeling sat with the door open every evening doing his homework in his boxers.

After everyone was checked in Sam would stop in to visit Theo. His apartment under the eaves was bachelor-Spartan, with big school-issue green leather armchairs and couch and nothing much on the walls. And, of course, it stank of cigarette smoke. Sam would tell Gibson some of what he'd noticed on patrol and they'd have a few harmlessly conspiratorial laughs at the expense of the young'uns. Theo listened to Sam's monologue about the other boys with a cocked eye—tolerant and amused, missing nothing. When they talked about Sam's own work, though, he gave no quarter, calling him out when he was lazy or careless, hectoring him when he slacked off. Over time, though, Sam had come to feel that Gibson was encouraging about his prospects; in spite of everything he knew about Sam's failings, Theo, he was sure, was in his corner.

One night while they were gabbing, Gibson said, "Your poem was remarkable, Sam."

Sam had shown him the long poem he'd dedicated to Eddie, his senior English project in George Tremallo's 4S. He'd spent weeks on it, typing up drafts on his aunt's old Olivetti portable with its aged blue ribbon and dirty keys, cutting and pasting the sections before mimeographing it for the class. "Gilgamesh Becomes a Man" summed up every-thing he'd felt and thought in his three and a half years at Leverett. It wasn't so much about Eddie as it was addressed to him, a series of bone-dry Eliotic vignettes in the voices of identifiable Leverett types. Eddie was the hero, the embod-iment of youth, health, and action who had saved Sam from a desiccated future as a repressed schoolmaster, setting him free into the arms of a girl far more elusive and featureless than Eddie's Sally, because she was totally made up.

Sam blushed now at Theo's praise. "I did work on it," he allowed.

"It certainly showed. But even more than the writing, it was your courage that struck me."

Sam didn't know what to say.

"Some things are almost too hard to talk about, aren't they?" Theo went on, rescuing him. "There are times you can put things down on paper when you can't otherwise find words for them."

"I imagine that's true."

"Braddock has always struck me as ... an original," Theo added. "He's not a happy camper, is he?"

"I ... I can't speak for him," Sam stammered, embarrassed and proud that their relationship was under discussion.

Eddie had made a large impression that winter, on everyone. Kaiser and Sam were coeditors that year of the student magazine, *Tterevel*—known to all as *T-terrible*. Sam had never had the courage to submit anything beyond an essay or two, but Kaiser and Darman and a few others were frequent contributors. There was an annual competition for the best story, which had been judged this year by Theo and Mr. Tremallo, and the winner, to everyone's surprise, not least Sam's, had been Eddie's story, "Repossession," a brooding Faulknerian tale of a man and his daughter living alone in a cabin deep in the backwoods of the Olympic Peninsula. As far as he knew, it was the only story Eddie had written.

"He suffers, I think ... like, like all of us. Maybe more," Sam ventured lamely. "I don't think he really knows what he wants."

Gibson stubbed out his umpteenth cigarette. "Ah, yes, adolescent suffering!" he said, with a wry smile. "There's no more powerful emotion. I hope you're enjoying every minute of it, both of you. Because it doesn't last, sadly."

"Mr. Gibson, I . . ."

Gibson threw his head back against his chair and turned to him, gently shaking his head. "Carpe diem, Sam, as the poet said. Go for it. Or it'll sail right by you."

Sam stared at him, stunned and ashamed. He wanted to ask so many things about this love of his—why he felt so alone in it, where it was taking him, how he was going to survive it. His left brain told him it wasn't everything and wouldn't last forever, but he couldn't afford to believe it.

Eddie wasn't coming to Harvard with them. They'd talked about rooming together and Sam had imagined it as the one way they could test their relationship—or, at least, that he could try himself in the crucible of Eddie's constant presence. He had red dreams of consummation, of blissful, uninterrupted togetherness, but he feared a fatal showdown, too, a conflagration that would lead to annihilation, with only emptiness beyond it.

Instead, Eddie was going home to Seattle to be with Sally. "I hate the East Coast, Brandt," he told Sam. "I don't want to be on the Leverett treadmill to law school and two-point-four kids in Westchester. You all think the world revolves around you. You have no idea what's out there."

It was true: Sam had no idea what was out there. His world had been here, with Eddie, and he couldn't see beyond it.

What he wanted more than anything that night was for Theo to give him a guide that would lead him through the looming inimical future. Instead, he got up from his chair, they shook hands, and Sam said good night.

THAT SPRING THE THREESOME, as Sam had come to think of Darman, Kaiser, and himself, prevailed on Gibson to lead them, along with their classmate Suleiman Baradi, in a seminar on Auden, Spender, and the English modernist poets. They invited Eddie to join them, but he refused to be part of such a pretentious undertaking. "You guys go ahead and jerk off all you want about Art and Literature," he told Sam. "Johnny and I will be right here waiting to pick up the pieces."

Twice a week they met after dinner in the room at the top of the Tower, which was furnished with couches and arm-chairs instead of desks. They huddled in a circle or lounged on the threadbare Turkey carpet, read poems, and argued about Marxism and versification and their emotions while the spring air wafted in through the open windows.

> *Does it look like a pair of pyjamas,*
> *Or the ham in a temperance hotel?*
> *Does its odour remind one of llamas,*
> *Or has it a comforting smell?*
> *Is it prickly to touch as a hedge is,*

Or soft as eiderdown fluff?
Is it sharp or quite smooth at the edges?
O tell me the truth about love.

They had intense debates about the inner life and life in the world fueled by their book-fed notions of conflicting loyalties and their own deep reservoirs of experience. They thought they were the cat's pyjamas, looking down through the newly opened leaves onto their benighted schoolmates listening to the radio or tossing a Frisbee back and forth on the finally green-again lawn below them.

Theo played along, encouraging their self-approbation.

"So tell us, Dave," he'd ask, his voice oozing mockery, "what *is* the truth about love?"

And Darman would answer, just as insolent, "'Love,' Theo, is no more or no less than unrequited lust. Everyone knows that."

"Do they now. So love is just an infernal inconvenience, no more than an irritation? Is that what you think, Baradi— an itch you scratch and be done with?"

"I have no idea," Suleiman answered in his fastidious Empire accent, giving up nothing as usual. "Never having been in love."

"I'll buy that," Darman sniffed. Suleiman, a willowy, imperturbable, exquisitely mannerly Iraqi, had never shown the slightest interest in Dave.

"What about you, Sam?" Gibson turned and asked him. "Can you tell us the truth about love?"

Sam knew what love was, all right—the burning, the self-abnegation, the sleeplessness brought on by unrelieved obsession. He was the chump who actually believed the poems and pop songs and old nostrums. He knew what love was, far too well, but, though he was capable of throwing caution to the winds and reading his poem for Eddie in Mr. Tremallo's class, he was too wary to expose himself to this carnivorous little crowd. He shook his head and lay there with his head cupped in his hands staring at the chandelier. *Besides*, he told himself, *they all know what I think. They pity my enthrallment.* Unless they secretly envied his belief in the romantic notions the rest of them claimed to be far too worldly-wise and jaded to subscribe to.

At one point Kaiser, his sarcasm masking what Sam knew was genuine curiosity, asked, "And what about you, Mr. Gibson? Won't you tell us the truth about love?"

"Not on your life," Theo answered with a snort. Then he added, "Everyone's recipe is different. Isn't that what Auden is saying? There's no general truth about love; there's only one's own."

Those spring evenings in the Tower might have been their last truly innocent hours. It was their final moment in the cocoon where they'd been allowed to develop without outside interference, basking in their God-given specialness, hanging back a little longer from the indifferent world where they knew they'd soon find out what they really amounted to. They learned nothing on those nights, nothing measurable anyway. But Sam never forgot a word of what they said.

And then it was June. It was over. They'd never be together again.

ON HIS LAST VISIT TO GIBSON'S apartment the night before graduation, Sam asked him to write in his *School Book*, as everyone had their friends and favorite teachers do. They'd shaken hands formally and embraced quickly, and then Sam had fled.

When he looked at what Theo had written back in his room, he was surprised to find it was in Latin. "*Cuius preti amor?*" it started, "What price love?" and went on for several lines that were too complex for him to make immediate sense of. Next to it Theo had drawn a cartoon of himself with a body shaped like Baba Yaga's house, with claw feet, a cigarette dangling from his lips, and smoke coming out of his ears.

Sam never took the trouble to sit down and work his way through Theo's message. It felt like an intrusion, a burden. He assumed Theo was offering him one last lesson from their seminar, maybe some kind of cautionary comment about Eddie, that he could do without. He'd get around to it later. Somehow, though, he never did.

EDDIE AND HE WENT DOWN to the river together early on the morning of graduation. The birch leaves were still not quite fully green but there was a breeze just barely troubling them, rippling the water. The sun was fully up though, already climbing the sky in these, the year's longest days.

Eddie sat on a bench by East Bridge and Sam laid his head in his lap for the first and last time, jagged with sleeplessness and grief. Eddie's chatter was willfully chipper and inconsequential, but Sam could hardly speak. *I know I'll live without you*, he said silently. *I just don't know how.*

They held each other in a long, silent, final embrace. Then it was up the hill to meet each other's parents—Eddie's didn't seem anywhere near as cold and threatening as Sam had imagined them, but genuinely kind.

They signed their friends' yearbooks and sat through the long, sweltering ceremony, mounted the platform and received their diplomas, returned their rented gowns and mortarboards, and then got into their cars with their irrelevant families and left Leverett once and for all.

Sam slept on the drive home, knocked out by exhaustion, exhilaration, misery. The future had arrived and torn them apart. Everything from now on was aftermath.

THE THREESOME MOVED ON to Harvard along with forty-eight of their classmates, just the way Sam's father had pictured it. They didn't literally sweep across the Yard in phalanx in their tweed jackets and loafers, but all the same they laid claim to the place as if it belonged to them—which, in a way, it did.

The dorms in the Yard were essentially no different from Leverett houses. They were red brick instead of yellow, a century or two older in some cases, but with the same dingy stairwells, the same triples carved out of doubles, the same bluff camaraderie among the inmates. The proctors, mostly debauched old preppies themselves, were charged with initiating them into the rites of adulthood. Harvard had already gone coed. A tie on a bedroom doorknob meant "Do Not Disturb."

They made forays into new territory—drinking, marijuana, acid rock, acid. Many, Sam included, found their first girlfriends. They explored the Square, still so much scruffier and more louche than the chain store mall it would soon become. Boston's Combat Zone, with its bars and theaters and strip clubs, was eight minutes away on the T. Sam went one evening to hear the Temptations at Symphony Hall and found he was one of the few whites in the crowd. He went another time with friends to see Martha and the Vandellas at a club and sat so close he could see the sweat streaking their makeup.

Slowly, they fanned out on their own. Sam thought of himself as a poet and fell in with a bunch of literati who hung around the *Advocate*. Darman gravitated toward the Loeb, where he was soon acting in and writing plays. They'd surprised everyone, themselves most of all, by rooming together. If there was anyone Sam was more unsure of, he couldn't have said whom; but keeping Dave close somehow seemed like the safest course of action. He was gone most weekends, driving down to New York—his mother had given him a car for graduation—or to Leverett to see Sandy. Occasionally, Sam went along to catch up with their old teachers, who endured their visits with stoic grace as if it were part of the job, knowing—and maybe even enjoying a bit—that the old boys hadn't quite cut the cord.

Sam dropped in once on Gibson, whom he found unchanged—brilliant, derisive, smoking up a storm as ever in his desolate attic.

"So how's the real world, Sam? How's work?" he asked.

"It feels remarkably easy—which worries me," Sam answered. Leverett boys often claimed freshman year at college was boringly more of the same academically. It wasn't till they became sophomores that the famous slump, the disorienting confrontation with enormous reality, set in.

"And love, Sam? Have you found out the truth about love?"

Sam shook his head. "I know what I know, Theo," he responded, calling him by his given name for the first time. He was tired of being taunted. "Nothing has changed." What hadn't changed was his grief, which was raw, despite the distractions of college. His missing Eddie, his sacrificial devotion, was the same as ever.

"A likely story," Theo responded, stubbing out another butt. "When the time comes, I expect a full report."

Why would I want to do that? Sam didn't say. Theo's interest in their post-Leverett lives felt ever so slightly prurient—not that he knew anything other than the few crumbs Dave and he let drop.

EDDIE CAME TO SEE HIM in Cambridge before Christmas, when the term was over and nearly everyone had gone home. Sam took him to meet his girlfriend Lena at her parents' house in North Cambridge. Lena, whom he'd met at a poetry reading in the Square, was still in her last year of high school and was stunningly intelligent and self-possessed. They drank Cokes and made stiff, spiky conversation like pretend adults in her parents' beige living room. Afterward,

Eddie told him she was "dry," put off, Sam surmised, by her confidence, her willingness to be argumentative. Little did he know how far from dry she was, how hungry for carnal experience that Sam had no way of giving her. She had a sweet, milky smell, a beautiful undulant body, and creamy breasts which she uncovered for him when they exchanged long kisses on her parents' wall-to-wall carpeting. Eddie thought she was dry, but Sam found her bewilderingly rich and earthy, and beneath their intellectualized conversation was an undercurrent he didn't know how to give her an inkling of having felt.

He felt it in Eddie, though. They went out and bought bread and cheese and illegal wine and holed up in Sam's room. Eddie lay shirtless on Sam's bed, his torso downy with little gold hairs, and there was alcohol on his breath when Sam kissed his warm, chapped lips. Sam saw the dark wisps under his arms when he turned away and wanted to lie there inhaling the sweetness of Eddie's sweat. But he didn't, of course, and eventually moved to Darman's empty bed, where he spent another night without sleep. The next morning Eddie flew to Seattle, leaving Sam more beholden than ever.

KAISER WAS ROOMING WITH SULEIMAN BARADI, their beguiling Iraqi Leverett classmate. Eventually Ray made his move, only to be predictably rebuffed, and the rest of their year together was full of awkward silence. Ray was pursuing another one of the Leverett boys, a coiled bantamweight wrestler who exuded a strong sensual whiff—but he, too, proved resistant to Ray's hard-to-pinpoint charms. Kaiser's acting out was becoming more and more extreme. He seemed to be heading off the rails.

Cambridge felt drenched in subterranean unhappiness. Maybe it was just Sam; other guys seemed to sail past it unawares, on their own quests for more socially sanctioned excitement. But for some the Square was a swamp whose rankness they were condemned to wallow in due to their morbid natures. The bathrooms at Widener, the big main library in the Yard, exuded a clammy, clandestine odor, as if perverse things were happening in the old blond-wood stalls (they were, he'd been told). And the sad turn-of-the-century apartment houses by the tram tracks west of the Square were magnetic in their rainy-day depravity.

The older brother of one of Sam's Leverett pals, one of the sweetest and funniest gay guys he knew, took him one rainy afternoon to meet Ed Hood, a defrocked graduate student who was a denizen of Andy Warhol's Factory in New York. They found Ed holed up with a pockmarked, long-haired guy who looked like an understudy for Joe D'Alessandro in *Flesh*. The shades pulled down in broad daylight, Ed's bunched-up yellow sheets, the streaked walls, the broken dresser, and general barrenness seemed like the perfect set-ting for the sins being enacted on Ed's bed.

Cambridge seemed drenched in sex—wrong, unhappy, haunted, haunting sex. It was reflected in the deep-socketed eyes of Boston's queer bard John Wieners, who lurked around the Grolier Bookshop on Plimpton Street, a musty, raffish clubhouse for poets of all persuasions. It pulsed in the lubricious soft-focus red-charcoal nudes of Laurence Scott, another former English graduate student whose enthrall-ment with male beauty seemed to rise off the pages of Wal-ter Pater and Oscar Wilde. Darman's mentor Dan Seltzer, head of the Loeb Theater, held smoke-filled all-male mixers in his Adams House suite on Friday nights. Sam was taken to one or two by a writerly type a year ahead of him who Sam could see was locked in resigned, unspoken love for an identifiably—to Sam at least—straight younger guy, a replay somehow of his own helpless adoration of Eddie. But Sam and his new friend never opened up to one another about their misery.

One evening he got a call from an anonymous man sug-gesting they meet. When he asked what for, the guy said, "What do you think?" then hung up with a muffled expres-sion of disgust. Later, on the wall next to one of the urinals in Lamont, the undergraduate library where he spent hours every day, Sam found a note in what looked suspiciously like Kaiser's handwriting that said, "For a good time call Sam," with his number below. When Sam confronted him about it, Ray exploded in raucous laughter. He thought it was funny—which it was, funny and cruel.

Before long, Ray had a kind of breakdown. He disappeared from Cambridge and cut off contact. When he returned the next year he was quiet, abstracted, as if tranquilized. They met every now and then but found they had little to say to each other. Darman moved off campus with a group of actors, and their connection, too, frayed.

Sam by then had fallen in love again and moved into Kirkland House with John and his roommates. The Leverett boys had faded from his life.

EDDIE HAD GONE BACK TO SEATTLE, enrolled in the university, and moved in with Sally. Sam hardly knew her, but they had something in common: they both loved this volatile character who seemed more and more determined to subtract himself from the world he'd known. Sam wrote him passionate, anguished letters into which he folded lovesick poems. Eddie as always answered some of them. Sam kept his whimsical, wandering notes in his desk, read and reread them in tears, and memorized them like scripture.

But he couldn't keep it up. One spring afternoon he lay on his bed under the eaves of Mathews Hall and wept because he knew he was letting go of his love. He fell asleep and woke still loving Eddie but prepared for new weather. The Yard was sunny. The clouds were barreling east. Darman was out on the prowl. Sam looked toward Thayer where his new friend John lived and, almost without thinking, let himself fall.

John had a boy's dewy, virginal appeal, a sidelong smile, and a mannerly come-hither reticence. And so, just like that, without thinking twice, Sam moved his chips from Eddie's pile over to John's and embarked on an enthralling, years-long, bound-to-fail quest for his often-professed but never-delivered love. John's impenetrable soft-around-the-edges straightness was the most desirable thing about him, and it was a formidable weapon in their game of alternating *fort/da* seduction and rejection. John was the new mountain Sam needed but would never be able to climb: precisely what Sam, and John, too, no doubt, wanted. His fixation would hold him in thrall for the rest of his time in college, semester after semester, girlfriend after girlfriend, and beyond.

HE WENT TO VISIT EDDIE in Seattle that summer. They took the ferry to the Olympic Peninsula and drove to his parents' house on the churning Pacific coast. Sam watched him catch sea trout in the chill water as the sun set, then grill them on a wood fire while they drank his father's scotch and Eddie extolled the brave world he was going to be part of. Later Sam lay sleepless in the bunk bed above him, choked with familiar, wordless, despairing love.

But he was already gone. He wept with humiliation and grief when they parted—humiliation at having been abandoned, grief and guilt at his own duplicity in abandoning Ed. He turned greedily to his new life with a steeliness he half despised. From Seattle he took the red-eye to Boston and caught a puddle jumper to Martha's Vineyard, where he spent a blissful week with John. Their thighs touched under the table as they ate dinner with his parents at the Edgartown Yacht Club. They became blood brothers the same night and lolled around in their underwear playing cards, holding hands across the space between the twin beds in John's room till they fell asleep. In the morning John got in Sam's bed to snuggle and gab, as he would for years, even after he was married. But that was as far as their bromance ever went.

EDDIE AND SALLY WERE MARRIED within the year. He sent Sam a framed picture of himself standing on a boulder at Big Sur, making the peace sign and sporting a bushy mustache. Sam sensed that psychedelics played a role in their lives. There were painful calls with teary professions of devotion, more wishful poems, another visit a couple of years later during which Ed sat shirtless again on the couch in Sam's room in Kirkland House and told him about his love for Sally, his leaving college to work as a newspaper photographer, his younger brother's death in a boating accident, the travails of his devastated family.

That summer he set Sam up on a blind date with his cousin Ruthie, and they spent a weekend with old Senator Braddock and his wife on their yacht in Nantucket Sound, ogling the Kennedy compound in Hyannis Port and mooring in Chappaquiddick Harbor on the night of the moon landing. A lot was going on with the senator and his wife on that boat, but not all that much between Ruthie and Sam. Mercifully, she looked nothing like Eddie, but the mere ghost of his presence was saltpeter for Sam. For a few months they exchanged letters filled with dutiful protestations of affection, but they gradually died out. His communications with Ed tapered off, too, and eventually stopped. They had little in common now except a few years that had hardened into a past.

Meanwhile Sam kept up his hopeless campaign for John's intermittent attention, which ran down like a played-out watch spring. Other men materialized—suitors, supplicants, aggressors. They were handsome, insistent, ingratiating, irritating, dull, but they weren't what he wanted: the one who didn't want him. He had a chaste flirtation with Tom Moutis, a graduate student who was engaged to be married but liked pinning Sam to the wall in his kitchen while explaining the intricacies of the various factions in the Harvard Strike that seemed to read back Sam's inner turbulence. Sam spent an evening smoking pot with him and another graduate student while Moutis hypnotically rubbed the other guy's stomach hour after hour.

He had girlfriends, too. They went to student plays and anti-ROTC sit-ins. They marched, wore armbands to class, and exchanged pro forma kisses. Finally, he lost his virginity to sweet, smart, far too understanding Martha; eventually he circled back briefly to Lena, too, still sensually out of his league. There were other girls he had feelings for as well, but they were always haloed by impossibility: too beautiful, too desirable, too entitled.

The August after graduation, not long before he was leaving to take up the fellowship he'd won at Oxford, he met Anne Dunning at a party given by friends who couldn't tear themselves away from Cambridge any more than he could. Anne was from Elsewhere: Iowa, a place untainted by Ivy League self-regard. Her acuity and her irony about Eastern pretensions were like an open window with a breeze agitating the curtains. She was elegant and demure, funny and interested. Soon he was interested, too.

Love with Anne was easier than anything he'd known before on either side of the line. And it was licit, sanctioned, welcome. For once in his life, he was doing what he was meant to do. They had their difficulties. But she was openhearted and understanding of his checkered history and they convinced themselves that with loyalty and mutual affection they could overcome almost anything. Ecstatic and relieved, Sam skated past the subterranean world he'd been eyeing and took off for two monkish years in England. They wrote and visited back and forth across the Atlantic, and by the time he returned he was ready.

Their friends were pairing off. He bullied Anne into following suit. They set sail together into the open waters of marriage and almost never looked back.

NOVEMBER
2007

THE LEVERETT DINING HALL, which sat on the hillside beyond the library, overlooking the river, resembled nothing so much as the basketball court it had once been. It was all blond wood: ceiling, walls, and floors. Ogive arches had been thrown up over the cavernous interior to suggest the hull of an old ship, but the ribs, which were hung with the pennants of victorious teams, only partly concealed its big-box outline. Cubbyholes crammed with backpacks, unpaired mittens, and lost schoolbooks crowded the entrances. What with the stench of old food, the steam from the industrial dishwashers, the gray glassware, it was hardly a place you'd imagine anyone wanting to linger, but there were corners, the alcove near the west door for instance, where some of the old-timers huddled together at suppertime.

Sam was finishing up with some old friends when Dean Harris, with his wife Sharon and their twins, stopped to ask him to take Dean's English 330 on Saturday morning, since he was going up to Hadley with the team.

"We're reading *Gilgamesh*," Dean told him. "Brotherhood, rivalry, sex, and the afterlife—all the best stuff. It's always good for a lively hour."

Dean was someone Sam found it hard to say no to. He was the rare contemporary exemplar of the old-fashioned boarding school triple threat: a challenging teacher, an inspiring coach, and an empathetic advisor in the dorm—an insufferable straight-arrow, really, except that he was also guileless, direct, and gentle, and liked and admired by almost everyone.

"How's morale?" Sam asked.

Dean smiled down indulgently. "You do know we're undefeated."

"Right." Sam affected to be ignorant of Dean's popularity as Leverett's assistant football coach. Dean pretended to rise magnanimously above his lack of interest.

"And what are you doing tomorrow?" Dean asked.

"Discussing *Gilgamesh* with your 330 and waiting on tenterhooks for the news from Hadley. And I have some work to do for Boris."

"You'll be the first to hear, I promise."

"Well, break a leg—each and every one of you!"

The Harrises moved off and Sam headed home. He knocked around the house, which still felt far too big now he was living alone. He called Frank and Eleanor and the boys at Hadley, but there was no answer. He even almost rang up Anne to gossip but thought the better of it. Finally, he trudged up to his study with a tumbler of scotch and pulled *Gilgamesh* off the shelf. Soon he was lost in it.

All of his body is matted with hair,
he bears long tresses like those of a woman;
the hair of his head grows thickly as barley,
he knows not a people, nor even a country.

It had been one of the books of his own adolescence: the first epic, about the Akkadian hero Gilgamesh and his wild friend Enkidu, the Jonathan to his David, who rescues him from the clutches of Ishtar but can't give him immortality.

He must have nodded off. He roused himself and made a cup of tea but fell asleep again and ended up spending a fitful, dream-haunted night on the couch.

ON MONDAY, HIS ENGLISH 210 SPENT third period working their way through Robert Hayden's "Those Winter Sundays":

Sundays too my father got up early
and put his clothes on in the blueblack cold,
then with cracked hands that ached
from labor in the weekday weather made
banked fires blaze. No one ever thanked him.

I'd wake and hear the cold splintering, breaking.
When the rooms were warm, he'd call,

and slowly I would rise and dress,
fearing the chronic angers of that house,

Speaking indifferently to him,
who had driven out the cold
and polished my good shoes as well.
What did I know, what did I know
of love's austere and lonely offices?

Sam loved the economy of Hayden's scene: the tension between generations in the house, the father's—and son's—"chronic angers"—what did the poet mean by "chronic"?—and the narrator's too-late appreciation of his severe parent's stoic devotion to his resentful son, his "austere and lonely offices" in strait circumstances. He was always curious what the kids would discover in the poem, how they'd relate it to their own lives. There was almost too much to say. Were father and son alone in the house? Why had the father polished the son's shoes? "Why does Hayden use the word 'cold' three times in fourteen lines?" he'd often ask, to get things going.

More often than not they worked their way to an understanding of the son's grieving empathy for his father, and how much these fourteen lines said about a relationship, a family, a world. But there could be days when the hour dragged as if they were stirring a bowl of too-dry cookie batter, and all of them, students and teacher alike, slunk away from the class-room dejected. Today had been one of those days.

Peter Reno, a new sophomore, hung back when the others filed out. He was one of the quieter kids in the class, tall for his age, with an aquiline profile, a freckled complexion, and disconcerting large, wide-spaced hazel eyes.

"How's it going?" Sam said.

"All right," he answered, a bit sulkily, but after a moment added, "Mr. Brandt, can I ask you something? What do you mean when you say 'metaphor'? You're all always throwing it around and I don't know what you're talking about."

"You mean like with the use of the word 'cold' in the Hayden poem today?"

"I guess so."

Reno often seemed distracted in class and he tended to sit by himself.

"A metaphor is a figure of speech, one thing standing for something else. It means a 'transfer,' a 'carrying over' in Greek. If I say, 'You're a long drink of water, Reno,' using the image of a nice tall, beaded glass of water to describe you, I'm bringing in a picture that's more telling than if I just said, 'You're pretty tall for your age.' It's the basis of all poetry, really: calling one thing something else to reveal something fresh about it. As we saw today, the 'cold' the poet is talking about refers to a lot more than the temperature in the house."

"I see."

Sam wasn't all that sure he did, but after a minute Peter said, "You're a peach, Mr. Brandt," with a big smile.

"I certainly am. Now don't you have somewhere you need to be?"

Reno left the room with a spring in his step and Sam suddenly felt a little better about the day.

HE MET BORIS as he was leaving Patterson and walked him over to Odegard House, the biggest and handsomest of the Federal houses on the town green, which served as the Head's residence. Once they were inside, he handed over Bryden's files.

"There's not a lot here," Sam told him. "A slightly below-average career, then a sharp downward slide in the spring term of third year. And an angry letter from the mother with a demand for the return of their deposit. Which the school agreed to. Highly unusual."

Boris raised his right eyebrow. "Who were his teachers?"

"Ebershof, Cerniak. Arrow. Gibson. Mastermeier." A cavalcade of Leverett's legends. Most of them had been Sam's teachers, too. They were two generations, really: The Grand Old Men who'd arrived in the thirties, when the school had benefited from Jedidiah Morse's enormous bequest and more than doubled in size. The way of teaching they'd developed— known as Morse Code in honor of Jedidiah's legacy, which by now amounted to more than a billion dollars—had become the school's calling card, its mantra, invoked day in and day out by Boris and his team. Then, in the sixties, the Grand Old Men had been succeeded by the Whippersnappers, who arrived trailing clouds of liberal revisionism; less hierarchical, more experimental in their pedagogy, less Old-Testament intimidating. Still male, of course, but not all stuffed shirts by any means. And, by that point, not all to the prep school manner born.

"What else do we have on Ron?" Boris asked, tossing the files aside.

"Not a lot, I'm afraid. He lived in Siberia, in Boughton House. Ran cross-country. I think he went to Tulane after Broadwick, but the trail goes cold after that. The alumni office didn't even have an address for him."

"Well, they do now. Ask them to find out what happened to him after college. Meanwhile, I'm going to invite old Ron for a visit."

"Are you sure that's a good idea?"

Boris was upbeat as always. "I think we can make him feel at home."

Sam shook his head. "You're the boss."

Boris was probably right that an application of Krohn's oil, as Sam and his pals liked to call it, would go a long way toward salving Ron Bryden's wounds, whatever they were. He'd be just as glad, though, not to have to watch.

BRYDEN ACCEPTED BORIS'S invitation almost immediately, and just after Thanksgiving he and Lizzie asked Sam to join them at Odegard House for a get-acquainted evening.

Dinner was scandalously early at Leverett, six at the latest, given that the school day, especially for Boris, began well before dawn. By seven-thirty they were all sipping decaf around the fire in the Krohns' living room.

Ron struck Sam as prematurely old. His gut strained the front of his blue-and-yellow-striped shirt and he sported a gray handlebar mustache, an unconvincing comb-over, unpressed chinos, and leather sneakers. It was hard to imagine him having been the object of anyone's lust.

They'd heard all about the ins and outs of the Tulsa bar and Ron's second marriage to a real estate agent who'd taken him to the cleaners. But when Lizzie offered seconds on coffee, Boris made his move.

"Ron, it's been wonderful visiting with you, and I want to thank you for making the trip back to Leverett," he said. "I'm wondering how the place strikes you today, compared with the school you remember."

"Well, Mr. Krohn, I'd have to say it hasn't changed at all."

"Really!" Lizzie exclaimed. "That surprises me. I mean, ten, no twelve buildings have gone up since you were here. And the student body has to look different. For one thing we've been fully coed, students and faculty, for decades."

"Sure, sure." Ron was dismissive. "But it still reeks of the goddamn old boy network. The same plaques in the hallways advertising the moral superiority of the top students. The same pie-faced portraits in the chapel. The same old elitist Leverett ideology. 'We're the best and the brightest, the whitest and the rightest.' It makes me sick."

"Leverett *has* changed, Ron," Sam said. "If you like, I'll take you on a walk tomorrow. You'll see that we're a pretty diverse institution these days. About forty percent are students of color. And a majority are on scholarship..."

"All well and good," Ron nodded. "Glad you're keeping up with the times. And how about the hallowed Leverett faculty? How rainbow are they? How many of them are still around, the ones who made my life a living hell?"

"There aren't many of the old-timers left," Sam said. "Atkinson, Smee, Gibson—most of them have passed away. We're the graybeards now."

"Yeah, well, they can rot in hell as far as I'm concerned." Ron's voice was rising. "And to think you're one of them, Sam. Sam Brandt and Theo Gibson, God's gifts, corrupting the youth together. But you always were the golden boy, weren't you?"

Ron had struggled up off the couch and was tucking in his shirt. "I've had enough of this," he said. "I knew coming here was a mistake."

Before they could react he was out the door.

HE'S ONE ANGRY CUSTOMER," Boris was saying. "And envious, too—of all the attention Gibson lavished on you. I heard all about it, at mind-numbing length."

It was almost two o'clock the next afternoon. Boris and Sam were catching a late grilled cheese in the empty dining hall. Boris had called Ron before eight and convinced him to come to his office. He'd cleared his schedule and they'd spent the morning together. Bryden was finally on his way back to Tulsa.

"I find this hard to make sense of," Sam protested. "Ron and I hardly saw each other after knob year."

"According to him, Gibson was always throwing you in his face: what a brilliant student you were, what a solid citizen, what an all-around peerless human being. I'm sure I would have found it insufferable myself."

"This was forty years ago, Boris."

"To Ron it's as if it happened yesterday. And seeing you again just drove it home."

"I told you, you should have taken him to the Inn," Sam said. "But surely Ron didn't come here to bitch about me."

"He wants payback for something." Sam recoiled invisibly as Boris crumpled up his napkin and threw it on his plate. "Some wrong he feels was perpetrated against him—neglect, abuse, whatever."

Boris's cell phone was playing "La Marseillaise." It was Jeanne, patching in Melissa Schaumle, the trustee president.

"I'm off to Hong Kong on Sunday," he told Sam. "Whatever it is, we need to be prepared." He pointed at Sam. "I'm counting on you."

"Melissa! How are things in Santa Barbara?" Boris was grinning from ear to ear, nearly shouting to make himself heard. School heads are like stand-up comedians. They're always on, always allegro and ingratiating. Until they're not.

SAM'S PHONE RANG LATE one January evening, in the middle of an ice storm.

He'd had a rollicking time with the Poets, as he called the group of sparky young teachers he loved hanging out with, jawing about the work and the messy lives of their colleagues, their favorite writers, and their students.

"You do know what happened when Ted and Sylvia stayed over at the Eliots' in Kensington," Shelby Leaderman said.

"Was that the night Groucho came for dinner and Sylvia talked so obsessively that no one else could get a word in edgewise?" Laura Halstead chimed in.

"It seems the sheets were a hell of a mess. Valerie had them delivered to Primrose Hill by taxi."

Being with them was pure joy. Nothing made him happier.

"YOU'VE BEEN ON MY MIND ever since I saw you," Bryden said under his breath with no introduction when Sam picked up. "I never did thank the Krohns for dinner." He sounded unnaturally near, and morose, as if he'd been drinking.

"I'm sure they'll be delighted to hear you enjoyed it."

Ron lowered his voice, down to business now. "I got so hot under the collar I never really got to the purpose of my visit."

"Ron, Boris is eager—"

"Yes, but I don't know Mr. Krohn," he interrupted. "He's very ingratiating, very solicitous and all, but as far as I'm concerned he doesn't have a clue about my Leverett, *our* Leverett. The one we suffered through—or I did anyway. I guess things were different for you."

"Trust me," Sam said. "They weren't. But I don't understand what's eating you, Ron. I hope you don't mind that Boris showed me your letter."

"It's all right. But you have to realize it's incredibly painful for me to open up about this. I'm reaching out to you because you were there."

"Tell me what happened," Sam said, as patiently as he could.

Ron was silent. At last he began. "What happened is that one of Leverett's legendary masters . . . took advantage of me, if you can believe it. In his apartment. Right there in the dorm. When I'd gone to him for comfort and support."

More silence.

"I was having a really difficult time." Ron was whimpering. "I was as miserable as I've ever been in my life. And he was the only one in the whole place who showed the slightest concern. He was my coach and my advisor. He knew exactly what I was going through.

"One night I was over at his place and I started telling him how much I hated Leverett. How brutal it was. How alienated I felt from the other kids. I guess I started sniffling a little. "And that... *bastard* came over and sat down beside me on that little two-seater couch of his and put his arm around me. Which made me start crying for real. We hugged for a long time. I may have even laid my head on his shoulder, taking solace that someone actually cared. Finally I got up to leave and he got up, too. And he pulled me close to him and kissed me on the lips. And he reached his hand behind me and put it down the back of my pants and kind of shoved me toward him. I could feel him up against my front. He was hard. He had a hard-on. God! When I think about it I get chills even now."

"Ron, I'm so sorry. That was very, very wrong."

"I idolized him. I looked up to him. I came to him for reassurance, for guidance. Wisdom. And that's what I got. I don't think I've ever been able to trust anybody since."

Sam could hear Ron weeping on the other end of the line.

"This is terrible, Ron. Did you reach out to anyone?"

"Who? Not my parents, God knows. Or anyone in the administration. I never said a word about it, ever. Until I decided to write to Headmaster Krohn last fall."

After another pause he said, "I just want to ask you one thing."

"What, Ron? Anything."

"Did he do it to you, too?"

"Who?" Sam asked. But his stomach had already contracted.

"*What do you mean, who?*" Ron was shouting now the way he had at dinner. "You know *exactly* who I'm talking about! Theo Gibson is who! Did he do it to you, too, or was it just me?"

"Theo never touched me, Ron," Sam answered, as calmly as he could. "He was my...my teacher."

"He was my teacher, too—and that's what he taught me. He was always throwing you in my face. What an upstanding example of the Leverett ideal you were. How I ought to model myself on you. I envied you, I admit it. And I guess I was right to. It seems he saved the real stuff for you and gave me...something else."

"This is deeply troubling, Ron. I just can't believe it of Theo," Sam said.

"You can't believe it. I'm telling you the most difficult truth of my life and you're making excuses for him."

"Ron, I do believe you. It's just—it goes against everything Theo stood for."

"There you go with the old Morse Code bullshit! You're all so full of yourselves, so convinced of your brilliance and selflessness and virtue. You won't own up to the truth when it's staring you in the face. And you're just as bad as the rest of them, Sam, because when it comes down to it, you're one of them. Wouldn't Theo Gibson be proud! His star pupil. His son. His legacy. Do you diddle the boys, too, Sam? I always thought you wanted to."

"This is incredibly upsetting, Ron," Sam said. "It was a terrible betrayal."

"Yes, it was. And you betrayed me, too. You dropped me like a stone after knob year. And waltzed off into the sunset with your boyfriend."

"I'm so sorry about this, Ron. I need to tell Boris."

"I want something done. You'll be hearing from my lawyer."

The words of yet another apology were taking shape in Sam's mouth. But Bryden had hung up.

Lying in bed later, Sam asked himself if Theo could really have done what Ron had accused him of. It didn't jibe with his idea of Theo, who was always so caustic and cynical, and at the same time so attentive—if detached.

And what was Ron so envious of? That Theo could have been supportive of Sam at the same time he was taking advantage of a troubled, nerdy kid? Sam found himself wondering if maybe Ron had unconsciously—or even knowingly—encouraged what he said had happened.

He was doing it again: searching for ways to exculpate Theo—out of loyalty, was it, or because of his visceral dislike of Ron? How was he supposed to feel now about Theo's brilliance, his wit, his love of learning, his dedication to his students, his encouragement of Sam and so many others, in the light of Ron's story?

And his life in that cell of an apartment, his aloneness, his endless smoking...

Drifting off—it must have been well after three—he remembered something he'd failed to tell Boris in the run-up to Ron's visit, a story he'd heard from his colleague Tom Hargitai. Tom had been a year ahead of them in school. He hardly knew Ron, really, but he'd told Sam this:

"One night I'd been up working in Hollister. It was lights out at eleven, but there I was at my desk with a towel stuffed under my door, cramming for a test. And suddenly who do I see but Ron Bryden flying out the door, desperate not to be caught out late. Where was he coming from? The stairwell that led to the south entrance was next to Gibson's apartment on the fourth floor. My room on the second looked out over the door. Ron must have been at Theo's for a teacher-student conference that had run late. Gibson was such a stickler for the rules, though, that it didn't make sense.

"But I remember thinking it might mean something else when I saw Ron again a couple of weeks later rushing out the same door and heading home well after midnight."

THERE HAD BEEN HOMOSEXUAL masters at Leverett as far back as anyone could remember, though the issue had never been openly discussed. Boarding schools had always harbored—you might say, depended on—single men who could be counted on to live ascetic, self-abnegating lives outside the classroom. Some had other bachelor or female friends they drove down to the city with to museums and the theater or went on vacation trips with. Some were coaches, fixtures on the playing fields and in the locker rooms, deeply involved with the young athletes who embodied an ideal they passionately admired, presumably from a distance.

When Sam was studying at Oxford, he'd run into Tom Goodwin, a bachelor English teacher he'd known when he was a summer teaching fellow at Mount Moriah, Leverett's sister school on the other side of the river. Tom, who was spending a sabbatical year in England, invited him to drive down to Barcelona over the Easter long vacation. They stopped at Mont-Saint-Michel and Perpignan, staying in small hotels with just one *lit matrimonial* in the room. Sam lay as close as he could to his edge of the mattress, and Tom, needless to say, was gentlemanliness personified. Still, Sam felt ill at ease being given the once-over by the waitresses in the breakfast room the next morning. He felt half-dead around Tom.

Leverett had examples of its own sprinkled among the standard two- or three-child nuclear families of most of the faculty. Jean Boucher, whom Kaiser called Johnny Butcher, had been a young history instructor whose open admiration for a well-built wrestler meant that he and his long-haired chihuahua Chouette failed to return for a second year in his Hopkins House apartment, which Mr. B. had hung with floor-length silver satin drapes. Then there was Dominique Dunand, a gawky, myopic Ph.D. in French literature from Quebec, who'd arrived at Leverett after failing to win tenure at the University of Rhode Island. Dunand was inspiring in the classroom, one of Sam's favorite teachers, but he would literally drool flirting with the younger boys outside the dining hall or on the Oval. The objects of his affection were civil to his face, but they made cruel fun of him behind his back.

Dunand was patently queer, but it was inconceivable that he would ever have touched anyone. He was like the old choirmaster Freddie Ayers, so swishy that he was universally regarded as harmless. Dunand eventually left Leverett a couple of years after Sam graduated, moving on to a day school in Des Moines. There were others, though, whom it was harder to get a bead on. Gibson, for instance; demonstrably a loner, he was clearly drawn to kids he had nothing in common with. Why was it that someone as effervescent as Theo had chosen to teach at a lonely place like Leverett? Maybe a school full of adolescent boys was a force field he hadn't been able to acknowledge, even to himself.

He'd lived like a priest, really, confining his interactions with the boys to inconsequential banter in the classroom and sharp, always constructive criticism on the track or in the dorm. He'd been a true friend to Sam and scores of others.

Except, possibly, for Ron Bryden. *But why Ron?* Sam asked himself if it could have been love that Theo had felt for this lost soul. Had he ever loved one of his own students that way? It was human nature, wasn't it? Put warm bodies together in a sealed environment—a nunnery, a prison, a boarding school—and unnaturally intense attachments were bound to form. (Once the girls arrived, they'd immediately become the objects of these fixations, too.) He'd had crushes on more than a few of them, girls and boys; at their stage of life they radiated unfolding Eros, and the older they got the more alluring and the more aware of their power they became. Some of them, consciously or not, broadcast a kind of ersatz availability, so eager, or was it desperate, were they to be recognized, valued, adored. Nor had he been above basking now and again in their dewy-eyed idealization. But they had always been another species, delectable but utterly alien. His vulnerabilities were different.

It was conceivable, though, that Theo Gibson—still young, single, cooped up with a brood of nubile young boys— had imprudently, pathetically, selfishly, and criminally given in to his passion, if that's what it was, for Ron Bryden of all people. And now everyone—everyone but Theo—was going to have to deal with the consequences.

THE PERSON WHO'D BEEN CLOSEST to Theo was Carla Van Ness, a legendary English teacher who was the senior Afro-American member of the faculty. Carla was statuesque, with beautiful emphatic features which she often accentuated with large gold hoop earrings and bright lipstick in arresting hues. Her repartee was instantaneous, vivid, and often cutting. On the rare occasions when Theo made an appearance in the dining hall, he'd scan the room at the entrance and make a beeline for her table, no matter whom she was with.

"What do you two talk about?" Sam asked her once, hoping he'd disguised his envy.

"Why, everything," she'd answered, then burst out laughing. "Absolutely everything!"

Carla and her historian husband Emil Higgins had been Leverett's first faculty members of color. They'd been hired by Mareike Crowley back in the early eighties, fresh out of Penn. Carla had a Ph.D. in English and a contract with a New York publisher. *Pot of Gold*, a book of linked stories about a dominating mother and two daughters based, Sam had been told, on Carla's own upbringing in the Southwest, had won a couple of first-book awards and become required reading, at Leverett anyway. Carla had been seen as one of the hopes of Black feminist fiction, along with Gayl Jones and Toni Cade Bambara. But, as with many before and after her, teaching at a boarding school hadn't turned out to be compatible with artistic production. Carla had published a number of other stories over the decades, including one in the *New Yorker* in 1996, but her novel hadn't materialized. Not that it made a difference at Leverett; she was a superb teacher, popular with the students and admired, if sometimes feared, by her younger peers. But she'd stopped talking about her own work years ago.

In their early years Carla and Emil had put up with a lot from the old-timers, who would have strenuously denied that they considered them anything but exciting new colleagues, but whose passing remarks could suggest otherwise. "We do it this way," they were advised, about everything from how to teach a class to what to wear in the dining hall. Emil appeared to take it more or less in stride, but it wasn't long before Carla let it be known she'd be doing things her own way. Over time, the cadre of faculty of color had grown substantially, but it would be an exaggeration to say they fit seamlessly into Leverett's insular culture. Carla had been their mainstay, showing them by example how to make their way.

Carla displayed her difference from her environment—her color, her sex, her tastes and convictions—like military medals. It had been a long-drawn-out engagement, but it was clear to everyone that she'd won. Her popular classes were open forums of debate, and her students were consequently often the best writers in the school. Her interventions at faculty meetings, which had been known to last up to half an hour, were delivered with such cutting precision that it was a foregone conclusion she'd carry the day, whatever the subject.

In her thirties, she divorced Emil, who left Leverett, soon remarried, and went on to a distinguished career at Saint Savior, a Catholic day school in Southport. Carla had grown close to Myra Broderick, the dean of students, and when Myra was named Head of School at Brooklyn Friends she asked Carla to come along. But Carla had stayed put, in spite of her jaundiced view of some of her monotone, not to say provincial, colleagues. Over time she'd become a Leverett legend. Carla Van Ness was one of the school's calling cards, along with Morse Code, the math department, and the Blagden Library.

Sam had never been entirely comfortable with Carla. She was always cordial, and always reserved. They'd only truly connected once, when she'd gotten into an argument with Andy Halliburton, one of the oldest of the Old Guard, about a student he thought was acting confrontational in class. Sam had always found the girl engaged, if outspoken, and defended her, and Carla backed him up. Andy never said another word about Gloria Watkins. But solidarity with Carla that afternoon hadn't translated into friendship between her and Sam. They were like-minded professionals, nothing more.

He stopped into the English faculty room on the first floor of Patterson after class one day and found Dean and Carla and a couple of their colleagues shooting the breeze.

"Did I mention Daphne Homans' paper on Sappho and Anne Carson?" Dean was saying. Daphne was one of Dean's advisees and, it was clear, his current favorite.

If the kids knew how keenly the faculty followed their fortunes, like two-year-olds at the track, they'd likely have been more than a bit self-conscious. Instead, most of them kept their heads down and worked away as if they were next to anonymous. Not Daphne, though. Somehow, she knew how good she was.

"Daphne is an absolute dream," Carla told the room. "The lip on that girl is remarkable. Her articles in the *Hutch* about intersectionality and student alienation have been *incandescent*. The administration has noticed. And they're not pleased."

Carla had long been the advisor to the student paper, which was a perpetual thorn in the side of Boris and his lieutenants in Main. Daphne would make a great journalist someday—or maybe a Supreme Court justice. For now, she was honing her investigative skills at Leverett, and Boris was a prime object of her scrutiny. She had no hesitation asking him inconvenient questions about administration policy that he had no intention of answering.

"Well, let's try to keep her on the straight and narrow," said Dean. "She's got a ways to go."

"I say, let her rip," Carla answered. "We need a little excitement around here. I'm bored." Everyone laughed, Dean included.

Dean had been at Leverett for more than ten years now, but unlike other younger instructors who were prep school alumni themselves, he had a broader outlook—less entitled, and in Sam's eyes more imaginative.

He'd grown up in Meriden, half an hour south of Leverett, where he'd been the high school quarterback, and had been hired at Leverett as assistant to Frank Forgione, the varsity football coach. He'd studied English on a scholarship at Wesleyan, and had written a memoir about how life had gone for some of his friends who'd stayed at home, dedicated to the memory of a cousin who'd died in Afghanistan, that had been published by a small press in New Haven. Dean had known his wife Sharon Dwyer since junior high school, and they'd married after college. She taught English, too, at their old alma mater. They had twin daughters just entering their teens.

Dean and Carla had made common cause in the Leverett English department wars. He and Sharon and Carla were family, really, going back to their days sharing dorm duty in Wells Hall. Dean's reasoned straight thinking was the perfect foil for Carla's intuitive assertiveness. Their Punch and

Judy show was effective because it was so disarming. The politician in Sam was full of admiration.

HE INVITED THEM ALL to dinner one Saturday in March. Carla arrived wearing a form-concealing tent dress, orange-and-black batik, with her signature earrings—for Lent, she said. She usually wore her hair down, but tonight it was piled luxuriantly on top of her head. It gleamed like copper, reflecting the blaze in Sam's living room hearth.

The conversation got around to Daphne's latest editorial in the *Hutch*, a merciless takedown of Boris's plan to revise the daily schedule. Sam thought Daphne's attack had been over the top, but not Carla. Her disdain for Boris was long-standing, starting with his promise, often renewed but never acted on, to ensure that faculty and staff of color became full-fledged members of the Leverett community. To Carla, Boris was a bag of hot air whose real interest was maintaining the status quo. And Daphne, she was convinced, saw right through him.

"I wonder what Theo would have thought of Daphne," Sam said.

Carla took the bait right away. "He would have absolutely adored her. If anything, she's even more acerbic and cynical than he was—and she's only fifteen. Too bad she's not a male. He would have been in *love*."

"I never knew Theo was one of the boys," Sam said.

"Didn't you now." Carla lowered her head and looked at him askance. "Well, he didn't talk about it, for obvious reasons."

"Do you think he might have had another life off campus, in Springfield, maybe, or Hartford?"

"Theo?" Carla scoffed. "Are you out of your mind? He was either here with the kids or in Worcester looking after Eufemia. Talk about a piece of work! There was simply no time for anything else."

"I kind of hoped he had," Sam murmured. "He seemed so solitary."

"Yes, Theo was a loner through and through. But they're used to it, you know, those hardy souls who embrace the Love That Dare Not Speak Its Name out here in the boonies. In fact, maybe that's why they come in the first place: to be alone. Alone With Their Pain." Carla put her wrist to her forehead and leaned back like Garbo.

"That really dates you, Carla," said Sharon. "Self-denial is for the birds these days. You know that."

"Boy, do I," said Carla. "Which is one of the few reasons I'm glad I'm the age I am. People today don't know what deviance *is*. It means you're not *like* everybody else. It's not a dress you get to put on and take off, something you *choose*. It's who you are. It defines you. It used to have consequences. Nowadays, everybody wants a place at the same boring blond-wood table. Adam and Steve are raising their little replicas, joining the PTA and baking cookies for the church fair. I say, Fuck that, pardon my French. Can you imagine Theo in a *relationship*? The man was a celibate, a monk. I respected that. I got it."

After dinner, Sam brought out his collection of digestifs and they all had something, the ladies, too—a first in his experience.

"I hear there've been some questions about Theo," he said, keeping at it.

Carla was immediately on the alert. "What kind of questions? And who's asking?"

"I don't know. Boris is looking into it," Sam said.

Carla turned away. "Well, you can tell Mr. Krohn I have less than nothing to say on the subject."

A couple of years ago, in his early seventies, Theo had abruptly retired and, to everyone's shock, died a few months later. The exact nature of his illness had never been made clear, but once he'd learned he was sick he'd totally withdrawn. The community was stunned by his disappearance. They felt shunned, judged, wronged by not having been allowed to be involved in his passing.

Carla had been the one to find Theo in the Jackson Street house, after he hadn't returned her calls for several days. He was in the bathroom, naked on the floor, icy water still in the tub—a heart attack, according to the coroner's report. She had been Theo's executor. His modest estate, apart from a few bequests, had been divided between the classics and English departments.

Soon enough the wound would close. He'd be absorbed into Leverett mythology and slowly forgotten. But the sense of something unfinished, uncelebrated about Theo's life hovered over his memory.

Carla stood up now, kissed Dean on the top of his head, and moved toward the door, taking Sharon along with her. Before leaving, she turned and said, "I was awfully sorry to hear about you and Anne, Sam."

"Thank you, Carla. I know you know what it's like," he answered.

"I do indeed."

Carla had been enraged when she'd discovered that Emil had been having an affair with Denise James, one of their friends at Mount Moriah, and she'd broadcast her unhappiness far and wide. Eventually, though, she'd stopped talking about the breakup. They hadn't been right for each other, was all she'd say when the subject came up.

THAT WAS KIND," Sam said to Dean once they were gone. "I was hoping for a bit more about Theo, though."

"That's no way to get the goods from Carla. You have to woo her a little. The truth is, she's as loyal as they come."

"I guess I always feel so utterly square when I'm around her."

"You are square, Sam," Dean said. "You just need to accept it the way the rest of us, Carla included, did long ago."

Sam sighed.

"And how well did you know Theo?" he asked. Dean had hardly spoken all evening.

"Through her, mostly. He'd drop in at her place every now and then. There were some late evenings in the early years. For someone who was notoriously testy in the classroom, he could be the life of the party, especially with Carla around. I liked him," he allowed—a little reservedly, Sam thought.

"By the way, if I can say so," Dean added, "you're looking pretty hale, all things considered."

"I'm relieved you think so," Sam answered. "I've been worried you might be worried about me."

"I have been. Which is why I'm glad to see you're okay."

Sam thanked him and showed him out. He stood on the stoop watching as Dean headed toward the Oval.

Talking with Frank on the phone one night, he asked, "You remember Theo Gibson, don't you?"

"Of course. I never had him in class, but Danny did." Daniel Wintersteen, a gangly redhead from Philadelphia with a mouthful of braces, had been Frank's best friend all through Leverett.

"And?"

"He loved him. Thought he was absolutely brilliant. Maybe a little terrifying, a bit . . . intense."

"How so?"

"I really don't remember. Do you want me to ask him?" Danny was working out West these days but he and Frank were in frequent touch.

"Do. And let me know what he says."

"What's this all about, Dad?"

"Oh, not much, really. Ancient history."

Frank snorted. "You are such a bad liar. What's the matter? Did Theo turn out to be an embezzler, or a pervert? Didn't you have him, too, back in the Dark Ages?"

"I did indeed. And I thought he walked on water. I'd be interested to know how Danny saw him."

"I'll get back to you."

FRANK HAD BEEN BORN at Hadley during Sam and Anne's tour of duty there, and he'd met Eleanor, whose mother had retired the previous year after twenty years as Principal, in kindergarten. The school is built around a group of roomy red barns set among orchards that seem to stretch up to the Green Mountains. Winters are cold and bright and empty. Tousled hair, ruddy cheeks, long johns: a more wholesome way of life it's hard to imagine.

After Swarthmore (Frank) and Bryn Mawr (Eleanor), they got married and went north again, he as a math teacher and lacrosse coach while she taught biology and coached tennis. The boys were six and four now—third-generation boarding-school inmates, God help them. None of their parents or grandparents had ever signed a lease or paid a utility bill. How were they going to cope, Sam often wondered, in a world of identity theft and driverless cars?

Frank was a man of flawless competency and application, and Sam was proud that he'd chosen to follow in the old man's footsteps, though the English teacher's navel-gazing was not for him. Like most of his generation, he was far more involved with his children than Sam had been with him. He was also, to tell the truth, a bit stolid and withholding, at least with his father. Even more than Sam, Frank was a man of few words. As a teenager and young adult he'd been tense and standoffish, though Anne usually knew how to break into his solitude, even if it meant raised voices and slammed doors. As adults he and Sam had settled into a measured cordiality—a little careful, perhaps, but they were father and son, after all. Frank was unfailingly polite the way Sam had been with his own father; Anne had called him dutiful, which wasn't a compliment. Frank would have probably said that they had so much in common they didn't need to spell things out. From his hawklike profile to the way he dressed to what he did all day, he looked and acted for all the world like a chip off the old block. Only he and Sam knew how much this wasn't the case.

F and E's marriage was a partnership. They divvied up responsibilities into Column A and Column B and were punctilious, not to say Jesuitical, about fairness. It reminded Sam sometimes of how he and Alex used to hover over a piece of cake, with one of them doing the slicing and the other making his choice. Their visits to Leverett were straight out of Column B (Eleanor's parents had retired near Hadley, and they saw them all the time). As a rule, they stayed with Anne, but every once in a while they'd spend the night with him.

Loving the boys was easy. They lapped up attention— playing checkers, walking in the woods, going to games, being read to. And Eleanor knew how to serve up a fair approximation of daughterliness. But when they left on Sunday evenings the ache of what hadn't been said could be sharp.

Frank made it clear early on that he wasn't interested in delving into what had happened between his parents, and was meticulous about not showing favoritism in how he treated them, though Sam couldn't help sensing a new reserve in the coolness between them. It had been a bit easier, or a bit more real, maybe, with Eleanor. He liked her frankness—her directness, that is—and appreciated it that she took him aside when he was up at Hadley for a visit soon after he and Anne separated.

"I have to say I think what you're doing is weird," she told him while they were preparing dinner.

"I understand. All I can say is we wouldn't be doing it if we didn't feel we had to."

"I'm sure not. But it's hard to understand. Not for the boys, it just sails over their heads—for the time being, at least. But you and Anne had a life together: a family, careers, friends. I'm married to your son. How do you think it feels imagining he might pull up stakes thirty years from now?"

"Frank knows himself far better than I ever did," said Sam. "He's always been more mature than I am—he's an only child, after all." He added after a moment, "I can only hope that someday he, and you, and the boys, too, will come to see that in the end you can only be who you are."

Eleanor nodded slowly, then looked across the counter and asked, "How about a drink?"

The rest of the weekend was devoted to the boys.

SAM MET DEAN AFTER THEIR 5:25 class on a Monday and they walked downtown to the Rust Bucket. Normally, they talked about the kids, or how Leslie Sturdevant was running the department—ineptly, in Sam's eyes. Dean tended to defend her, but he had ideas of his own, about how the entire curriculum could be restructured, for instance.

"Have I told you what Daphne's been up to?" he asked as they poured out their Nutmeggers.

"Don't tell me she's an artiste now, too." Sam was feeling competitive. Peter Reno, his sophomore, had started writing, and some of his efforts weren't half bad. They had their own workshop Thursdays after dinner at Bixler House.

"I'm afraid she just might be. That girl..." Dean shook his head.

"Am I detecting a bit of a crush?"

Dean took a swig of his beer and wiped his mouth with the back of his hand. "Actually—I'm breaking a confidence here," he said, "but Daphne's the one who's in love, with her roommate, Abby Kumar. I wouldn't be surprised if she wrote about it in the *Hutch*."

"I can only imagine how that will go down with Boris and the deans."

"I've never had a student like Daphne. Not just brilliant, but confident, fierce. Okay, maybe she's a bit too sure of herself, a bit intolerant..."

"A bit...entitled?" To Sam, Daphne ran the risk of exemplifying the new breed of student with helicopter parents who considered the school just another service provider and expected to be catered to accordingly.

"Yes, all right. But she couldn't care less about the juvenile things her dorm mates do. She and Abby don't rub it in anyone's face but they don't hide their love for each other either. And the other girls are protective of them. They're in awe of their closeness."

"Imagine how the faculty would have dealt with a student love affair in my day."

"Yes, but you're antediluvian, Sam. We're so much more self-actualized today."

THIS WAS WHAT THEIR CONVERSATIONS WERE LIKE: Dean open and excitable, Sam more indirect and self-protective. Dean lacked the desire, or was it the capacity, to manipulate anyone, yet he had Sam and the rest of the world eating out of his hand. Everyone was drawn to him. They all wanted a piece of him, and maybe they wanted to ruin him a little, too, cut him down to size if they ever got a chance. Luckily, he seemed oblivious of their envy.

But Sam wasn't just admiring of Dean; lately he'd become hyperaware of him, much as he tried to ignore it—of his looming presence, his voice, his long eyelashes and clean scent. His gait was hypnotizing; the way his chest hair forced its way through his open collar was stunning. All Sam wanted to do was be around him: to hear him talk, to have him answer his underhanded little goads and jibes with tolerant good humor and take him in with his even gaze.

Yet he often shied away from Dean because his effect on him was too strong. He'd started to fear Dean would sense his attraction and it would interfere with their closeness. He wondered if the Poets had noticed; how could they have failed to, being as perceptive as they were, though they were far too kind to mention it—even if Shelby had made a crack about how Sam always managed to find a way to sit with the Harrises in the dining hall.

What Sam found he couldn't and didn't want to do was hide what he was feeling from himself. When he had the chance, he'd get on his bike and go for a ride on the river road. He'd find an old maple to sit under, watch the water, and try to read, but he usually got no more than a few pages in his book before Dean's image would rise to claim his attention and the afternoon would be lost. But it wasn't just his age-old sense of being out of step and the anguish it aroused that was working in him now as it had in the past, it was joy that was turning him vague and distracted: joy to be alive again, no matter how pathetic he might seem to others, and himself. He was radiating openness, ecstatic to be suddenly feeling so much—and for another man. *You're a fool*, he told himself; but fool that he was, he was ecstatic to be one—though he didn't do anything about it other than seesaw between giddiness and heartache.

Dean mentioned Carla in passing now and Sam said, "I noticed you didn't say much the other night. I couldn't help wondering why."

"So you were watching me." Dean laughed but his eyes caught Sam's before veering away. Sam felt exposed, but he only frowned.

"I told you we used to see Theo at Carla's," Dean went on. "And later on we'd go over to Jackson Street every now and then."

"What was that like?" Almost no one but Carla had visited Theo there.

"Unlived-in, gloomy. And reeking, of course. I went by one night to talk about one of my advisees who was having trouble in Theo's 310. We had our chat, very to-the-point and professional. Theo was helpful the way he always was. He'd taken the measure of this girl and her issues perfectly and had ideas about how to get her back on track.

"But here's the thing: as I was leaving and he was helping me on with my jacket, he started massaging my shoulders, very deliberately. Neither of us spoke, and I moved away as if it hadn't happened. It could almost have been nothing—but it wasn't. I've never mentioned it to anyone, not even Sharon."

"How did you feel?"

Dean frowned. "Theo was a lonely guy. It was easy enough to shrug it off. But I did think it was strange that he could think it was okay to do something like that to someone he hardly knew."

"Thank you for telling me," Sam answered. "I have a Theo story of my own," he added, "though it's a bit different."

Sam had been a teaching fellow at Mount Moriah one summer during college. Theo showed up unannounced late one afternoon. They went and had a burger in town and then came back and lay on the lawn in front of the school-house. Sam had never seen him so relaxed: grinning, joking, not smoking for once. He stretched out on the grass with his hands behind his head and they talked about summer school, his upcoming classes, Sam's hopes for the coming year, what they were reading. When it was nearly dark and the mosquitoes were getting really vicious, Theo stood up and dusted himself off. They shook hands and he drove back to Leverett.

"And that was that—our last talk, as it turned out," Sam told Dean. "We never wrote, we never called. I'd go back every now and then to see my favorite teachers but Theo was almost always away on weekends.

"I've wondered every so often over the years what he'd been doing there, so relaxed and nonchalant," Sam said. "And then just...vanishing."

Sam remembered feeling a kind of shame when he thought of Theo driving back to Leverett alone. Sam hadn't been able to crack the shell of Theo's reticence. Or was it that he hadn't wanted to.

"Do you want to know what I think?" Dean asked. "He was looking for something. He realized it wasn't there and moved on."

"Do you think he ever came on to students?"

Dean's eyes widened. "Why are you asking?"

"Let's just say it's come up." He'd already said too much.

"God, I certainly hope not. All I know is that what he did with me came totally out of left field. He had no reason to expect it would be welcome. In fact, he must have known it wouldn't be. But that didn't stop him."

Dean was right. His story revealed a brazenness in Theo that nothing Sam had known about him would have led him to expect.

But he also realized he was feeling a kind of envy. Theo had found a way to make clear what he'd wanted from Dean. *Show, don't tell*, they were always telling the kids in class. And Theo had done just that. He'd shown Dean what he felt, what he wanted, without saying a word.

Eventually Boris convinced him to go see Ron.

"Ron's lawyer keeps making threatening noises. I'd like to see if we can head him off at the pass. You were there. You knew the players. See if you can talk him down out of his tree."

"What can I offer him?"

"Don't offer him anything. My hunch is that what Ron really wants is for us—and you, in particular—to acknowledge his suffering. He needs you to accept him as a brother, once and for all. You can do that, can't you, Sam? For the team."

If Sam and Ron were brothers, they'd been raised by different parents. What did they have in common, really? But there was no way he could say no to Boris.

It's not all that easy to get to Tulsa from Hartford. You have to fly to Charlotte or Atlanta and switch. It costs a fortune and it takes all day.

It was dark by the time he landed. He took a cab to the Holiday Inn downtown where they'd agreed to meet, but Ron called and asked Sam to come to his home instead. 3478

Madison was in the Maple Ridge neighborhood, about ten minutes away. The house was a handsome one-story brown-brick ranch, Frank Lloyd Wright Prairie style, shaded by old live oaks.

Ron answered the bell almost immediately and ushered him into an airy living room that wouldn't have been out of place in a shelter magazine, with shirred sea foam drapes and mid-century furniture. Sam was stunned by its elegance. The only thing that didn't fit was Ron.

"Ron, your house is lovely," he said.

"This was Alison's place, actually. When we divorced, I ended up with it."

"Well, it's wonderful."

Ron looked around him, as if for the first time. "Thanks."

He turned to Sam. "So, what's up? I imagine you're here on a mission."

Though Ron hadn't asked him to, Sam sat on one of a pair of couches in front of the fireplace. Ron took a seat facing him.

"I need your help. I'm trying to get to the bottom of all this," Sam said.

"My lawyer told me not to talk about it," Ron answered, arms akimbo. "Let the process take its course."

"I understand," Sam nodded. "But I'm not here about legalities. I want to have a heart-to-heart with you, off the record. Just between us. I promise you no one will ever know what we say to each other. This is for myself as much as anything. Will you tell me what really happened with Gibson? After all, we've known each other a long time."

"Yes, we have," Ron allowed.

"Remember when we went canoeing on the river and I tipped us over?"

"How could I forget?" Ron chuckled in spite of himself. "You were such a klutz."

"I always have been. Now help me, please, Ron. I can't tell who you're upset with, besides Gibson himself. Is it Boris? Is it the school? Sometimes I think it's me. What you've described was beyond reprehensible. Anyone with a conscience knows that. And Boris is anxious for Leverett to acknowledge its share of responsibility for what you say happened."

Ron's eyes narrowed. "*Its share*? Where are you going?"

"Someone—I can't say who—saw you coming out of Hollister all those years ago. Running home well after midnight. Late. Very late. And more than once."

Ron's back went right up. "I'd been playing poker with Lisle. We had a game every Tuesday."

"Till after midnight? I don't think so. You were visiting Theo. Admit it."

Ron stared at the carpet.

"I see," he said. "So you're blaming me."

"I'm not. I just need you to tell me the whole story."

Eventually he started talking.

"What I said was true. He assaulted me. It was criminal."

Sam nodded, eyes focused on Ron.

"But, yes, I did go back. We got into a thing. He was the only one who cared, it was the only tenderness I ever knew there. And so, yes, I did...let him. Sometimes he'd cry afterward. He'd hold me. He'd kiss my face and shoulders. He made us grilled cheese sandwiches and we'd have them in bed with hot chocolate. He helped me with my homework."

"How long did this go on?" Sam asked.

"A few months. It was all I cared about, the only happiness I ever knew there. Until we stopped. Or he did. He said it was wrong, that he loved me but he didn't want to interfere with my future. Interfere! I've never been so hurt in all my life. He dropped me. He took my...manhood and then, whomp! He shut the door and it was over, just like that. I'd see him on the Oval and he'd stare straight ahead as if I didn't exist. We never spoke again.

"And that's the whole truth, Sam." Ron looked up at him imploringly, his hands clasped between his legs.

"Ron, you were sixteen years old. It was unconscionable. Gibson said as much. If it happened today he'd be fired, prosecuted."

"Yeah, I hope he rots in hell."

"I can understand you feeling that way."

After a pause Sam asked, "So what should we do? Should we launch an investigation?"

"I'll have to think about it."

"Whatever you want, Ron. We can make a public report. Or…"

Ron stared at the floor. "You knew, didn't you?"

"I absolutely did not. How could I have?"

"I tried to talk to Braddock, but he brushed me off."

"He never mentioned it."

"I didn't exist for him. Or you. Or Gibson, either."

"I'm sure he was ashamed, tormented by what he'd done."

"That makes two of us."

"If only you'd talked to someone."

"Who? And what good would it have done? They'd never have believed me. Who knows if you believe me now."

"Ron, my heart goes out to you."

Bryden was silent. He sat unmoving, his head in hands.

"I'm going to go now," Sam said eventually. "Let us know what you decide."

Sam got up. He put his hands on Ron's shoulders and stood there silent for a moment. Then he walked out of his living room into the soft, still Tulsa night.

BRYDEN'S LAWYER WROTE a few weeks later that he was dropping his complaint against the school.

"I knew I could count on you," Boris crowed. He and Sam were sharing a celebratory drink at Odegard House. Boris liked a dirty Hendrick's martini on the rocks with extra olives and extra juice. Sam preferred Ketel One out of the freezer, straight up with a twist.

"I suspect the truth is that Ron has a soft spot for Theo, in spite of everything," Sam told him. "In some ways, maybe that's what it was really all about."

"What precisely *was* it all about?"

"I'm not sure, even now. I know what Ron *said* happened. Why don't we leave it at that? Think deniability, Boris."

"I wonder if we'll hear from him again."

"I would tend to think not. In fact, I'm willing to bet on it."

"My hero," said Boris, looking down at his BlackBerry, already on to the next thing.

"How well did you know Theo?" Sam asked as he nursed the last of his drink. Boris never offered a second.

"Not all that well. He was living off campus by the time I showed up. We had lunch on the run a few times. You may recall that he had strong feelings about maintaining the classical diploma, which I considered seriously..."

"Before letting it go," Sam said.

"...before letting it go. There just wasn't enough demand. Let's just say Theo was not a fan of my decision. And he was vocal in his opposition.

"Anyway," he said, rising, "I can't thank you enough. Truly."

But Sam wasn't ready to let go. "Did you ever think Theo might have been...odd with the kids?" he asked. "Did it cross your mind that he might be a problem?"

Boris set his glass down. "There are a hundred and twenty-three faculty members at Leverett," he said with a hint of irritation, "and they come in all shapes and sizes. Gibson never struck me as any odder than many of them. Was he any more...*unusual* than Carla, or Shelby Leaderman? Or Dom Dunand—to name just a few. People are idiosyncratic by nature, Sam. They can't all be like you, or me, or Dean Harris."

Boris ruffled Sam's hair as he guided him to the door. "We dodged a big bullet here, amigo. I can't thank you enough."

Boris was right in a way, Sam thought as he wandered home, not quite tipsy enough to fully bask in his boss's praise. Each of them had demons. They were all cracked, Boris included.

What was it that drove him? The truth was that Boris was not *echt* Leverett. He was still an outsider, even after his long tenure as Head, and always would be. It had allowed him a certain freedom of action at the beginning, when he'd come in brandishing his reformer's saber, slashing left and right like every new arrival. But what he'd really always hankered for, deep down, was to be inside. The Old Guard knew it and they used it against him mercilessly. They derided his rah-rah boosterism and mocked the way he sported the Leverett paraphernalia, not to mention his ridiculous mountaineer footgear. He registered their disdain without acknowledging it, always working to win their ever-elusive approval. He was responsible for preserving and protecting the Leverett way of life, after all, and he did it with a vengeance. But he was like the *diener* in a synagogue, the hired goy who would never be one of the congregation, because he wasn't.

LATER THAT SPRING he drove down to Trumbull to see his old friend Joshua Stern.

Joshua was a sculptor and a dedicated lover of men who'd spent his entire career at Trumbull College. His modus operandi, which worked beautifully for him, was to hide in plain sight: he made no secret of his sexuality—not that he could have—and boasted to anyone who'd listen about his copious liaisons over the years with colleagues and students and his rollicking online life. "Joshua is our Rabelais," one of their mutual friends liked to say, with a hint of resignation. His apartment across from the quad was a dusty museum of his conquests, overflowing with prints, photographs, drawings, and maquettes by and of guys he claimed had offered themselves out of gratitude, affection, curiosity—or, as he implied more than once, in satisfaction of a quid pro quo. It was all good fun to Joshua, or so he claimed. Sam, though, could remember his voice breaking when he told him early in their friendship about his passion for a beautiful, confused young man who clearly basked in Joshua's adoration but couldn't fully reciprocate his love. That seemed to be Joshua's recipe. He made it all seem lighthearted and carefree, but Sam was sometimes pierced by his solitude.

Early on they'd spent a lot of time together, often with a college friend of Joshua's named Dirk Brogan who was if anything more flamboyant than he was. Dirk was handsome in a way that might have struck many as effeminate, though he claimed to have lots of girlfriends. He and Joshua were like sisters, really, sharing outrageous, not necessarily verifiable secrets which they then competed in broadcasting to the wider world. After a couple of years teaching high school (he was fired from Mount Moriah for sleeping with a student), Dirk fell in love with a doctor in New Haven and settled into domesticity before dying of an AIDS-related infection in the late eighties. Joshua had soldiered on alone. He had scads of pals, an endless stream of hookups, and occasional boyfriends, too, notably in Rome, where he spent as much time as possible, extolling the pleasure-seeking freedoms that only a visitor could enjoy to the full.

Sam and Joshua had lost touch when Sam got married—not falling out, really, just drifting apart. But Sam had run into him at an art show in New Haven that winter and they'd had a boozy, confessional reunion. Joshua was the one person Sam felt able to talk to freely about what had been happening in his life.

THE SUMMER SAM TURNED FIFTY he'd had a mini-sabbatical and they'd chosen to spend it in Italy, at the house of Hadley parents who'd become friends, a *casa colonica* in the middle of eighty acres of olive groves on a hillside outside Arezzo.

It should have been paradise, but Sam was miserable. Here he was, deep into middle age, and where was he going? He loved his work, loved Anne and Frank, but a sense of something unfinished, unfulfilled, had left him feeling anxious and fraudulent. He'd felt exaltation and despair loving boys as an adolescent, but he'd barely put one toe in the water; he'd never gone all the way. Anne and he had something else—textured, reliable, gentle, not tormenting, not virulent. But the unlived life hadn't been supplanted by the life they'd lived.

There was a crew of workers putting a new roof on one of the barns on the property. The window in the room Sam was working in looked out across the farmyard at them, and one of the men, who was always shirtless, seemed to enjoy stopping whatever he was doing, taking a drink from his thermos, and staring long and hard at him before hiking up his pants and going back to work. This went on day after day. It was disturbing, and shaming.

He couldn't sleep that summer, couldn't work. He felt trapped in their idyll. He was irritable, cantankerous—impossible to live with.

And then it was over. Sam shook off his bad humor and they went home and were swallowed up in their lives.

But his fall depressions started returning. And his feelings for men kept asserting themselves, not so much in flare-ups or infatuations, though he had these, too, so secretly and sadly that he doubted any of his objects were even aware. It was more a melancholy that came and went, for years. He fantasized nonsensically about reconciling with John. Eddie was further out of reach, almost a ghost, but he dreamed about him, too. His feelings of failure and incapacity as the November light waned were insistent, unrelenting.

"I saw the way you were sitting with Shelby, leaning back in your chair as if you were hoping he'd kiss you," Anne said one night after dinner at the Sturdevants'.

She was wrong about Shelby. He'd never interested Sam except as a sparring partner. But she'd picked up on a frequency in him he hadn't fully recognized himself—though there had been a redheaded cashier at the IGA whose long looks he'd had to keep going back for more of.

Eventually, Anne found him online. Penny ante stuff, really—guys showing off the way so many of them like to today. But enormously shocking to her, and a definitive betrayal.

They had terrible weeks. Outwardly he was calm but he felt nauseous, tipsy.

"You came of age during the sexual revolution," she said during one of their long struggles to wring reason out of something there was no way to make real sense of. "Why didn't you figure yourself out then?"

Why indeed? And why now? she didn't need to add.

He was ashamed of his self-protective duplicity, his passivity and conformism, his lack of gumption.

They'd spent a lifetime collaborating, filling the mold they'd convinced themselves they were meant to inhabit. Their partnership had been the envy of their friends. Now they grieved separately and together for their shattered pretend peace.

In the end it was Anne who made the move. "I need more than this," she told him, more gently than she'd ever said anything, as he lay on the couch one evening pretending to read. "And you do, too."

Yes, there were nights that left them wrung out and hopeless. It had to be, given what they were letting go of. But that was later. Their fatal moment was surgical, anesthetized, and over in seconds.

What survived of their years together—beyond their devotion to Frank, their mutual loyalty, and the affection it continued to engender—was a sense of having failed at life's greatest assignment.

Anne had never liked Bixler House. She moved into an apartment over the bookstore downtown.

WELCOME TO THE CLUB!" Joshua exulted now, his eyes bright. "I thought this day would never come."

"There's nothing to get excited about," Sam objected. "Anne and I are separated, nothing more."

Joshua clucked. "That's what they all say. I say otherwise. You've made the leap. Now you've got to start meeting people. By which I mean men."

"And how do I do that?"

"I can introduce you. Or you can go online."

"You mean Match.com? I don't think I'm ready for that."

"Well, think again, bubbie. You're not getting any younger."

"Leverett isn't New Haven," Sam said. "Anyone who tried what you did back in the day would be out on his ear. And rightly so."

"No one has ever complained."

Maybe not. Sam admired Joshua's audacity and the unapologetic way he affected to revel in his outlaw nature. The shadow of his aloneness haunted Sam—but his desire for another chance, not Joshua's but his own, was stronger.

PETER AND HE WERE READING Allen Ginsberg.

"I don't understand what he means in 'A Supermarket in California' when he says he's 'shopping for images.'"

"Well, where is he?"

"In 'the neon fruit market.'"

"'Neon fruit market'—sounds a bit hyper-real, don't you think? 'What peaches and what penumbras.' Why do you think he decided to make it a fruit market?"

"Maybe because it *was* a fruit market, lit up by neon at night."

"Could be. Any other possible reason? Who's there?"

"Everybody: 'Whole families shopping at night! Aisles full of husbands! Wives in the avocados, babies in the tomatoes!—and you, García Lorca, what were you doing down by the watermelons?'"

"So, some pretty unusual customers in among everyone else. Sounds like he's having a vision. What else do they sell?"

"It's a supermarket. They sell food."

"And who's he speaking to?"

"Walt Whitman. He calls him a 'lonely old grubber, poking among the meats in the refrigerator, and eyeing the grocery boys.'"

"And why do you think Whitman is there? Might he actually be standing in for someone else?" Sam asked.

"You mean Ginsberg?"

Sam cracked a smile. "How does he describe Whitman?"

"He's a guide, a parent: 'dear father, lonely old graybeard, lonely old courage-teacher.' 'Which way does your beard point tonight?' he asks him."

"So…"

"So Ginsberg is trying to do what Whitman did, which is why he's 'shopping for images,' looking for ways to describe his vision of a whole messy multifarious neon-lit world."

"There's a here and now, the peaches, and there are penumbras, too, ghosts that are always with him. Peaches and penumbras."

"Yes. Fruits *and* meats. And Ginsberg and Whitman, and families and everyone. It's all a bit much, if you ask me."

"Isn't it? And isn't that kind of great?"

SOMETIME IN THE NINETIES, Sam had had lunch in the city with Darman and their classmate Albert Olson, who was in on a rare visit from Chicago.

It had been twenty-five years, but Dave didn't seem to have changed all that much. Maybe his features were more definitively set, his pout etched deeper but without too many crow's-feet, and no lines across the forehead. He was a little boxier, maybe, but still trim except for his always-outsize rear end.

Sam arrived a bit late and found them already at the table, talking about Dave's wife, Hella Moravec, a dealer in Incan artifacts he'd met in Lima and married a couple of years before. Albert had written Sam soon after the wedding to say how beguiling, how lovely she was. The move had surprised him, given Dave's history, but Hella, it seemed, knew all about his checkered pasts. Once again, Darman was demonstrating how ineffably square they all were.

Not that any of it had dissipated the jaded aura that had enhaloed him ever since he was a teenager. He was like that languid Blue Period Picasso of the boy with a pipe wreathed by a crown of roses—or is it opium smoke?—still glamorous, if several degrees less menacing. Which had something to

do, Sam suspected, with the fact that though panache and ambition had got him out the gate faster than the rest of them, Dave hadn't yet scored a palpable hit. Being a star high school thespian hadn't held water on or off Broadway, and despite the leg up he'd had from Paul Pleyel, who'd found him an agent and a job as an editorial assistant at *Esquire* for five minutes, his writing career had simmered along without coming to a boil. Darman had a drawerful of unproduced screenplays in his desk, no different from any number of writers who got paid lavishly for their unproduced work.

He and Sam had lost track of each other after college. At one point Sam heard he was working as a dramaturg in L.A. Then he'd gotten involved in repertory theater in the Canadian Rockies—not quite the starring role any of them had imagined for him, though interesting, worthy—similar in fact to what Olson and Sam and the rest of them were doing in their own ways. Darman the Terrible, it seemed, had more or less turned out to be one of them after all.

He was making a real effort to be friendly, maybe because Olson was with them. Albert got along with everyone, accepting or holding them at bay with measured geniality. He'd become a widely admired abstract photographer; but Sam felt another kind of admiration for him, in that Albert was the one among them who was genuinely kind.

"How's Pleyel?" Sam asked. Albert, he knew, had stayed close to Sandy.

"He's married again. He and Nicole have two daughters, five and three. They're living in Big Sur. Sandy's at Esalen, rethinking film from a Whole Earth perspective."

Sandy had turned inward. Where else could he go? Every furrow had been plowed for him by his prodigious father who, worst of all, had been impossible to resent. He'd been pinned, a perfect specimen of youth and potential, by his adoring, take-no-prisoners progenitor.

"I've seen him a couple of times here in the city," said Darman. "We hung out with his dad. Paul's well past seventy now. Though you'd never know it."

Sam didn't mention that he'd run into Pleyel at a MoMA opening some years before. He'd come up to Sam fresh-faced and sunny, stuck out his hand, and announced: "I'm Paul Pleyel."

"Mr. Pleyel! It's so good to see you again," Sam said, utterly startled. "I'm a friend of Sandy's from Leverett." They chatted about what Sandy was up to for a few minutes and then Pleyel moved on. Only later did it occur to Sam that Paul's approach might not have been merely conversational.

"I took Gibson over to Paul's studio recently," Darman went on (Sam was interested to learn they were still in touch). "His eyes were as big as plates. But they got along. It was almost like the good old days—though Theo's aged, too. But he's still pretty sharp, wouldn't you say, Sam? You're the one who sees him all the time."

Sam nodded. "He's still trouble, if that's what you mean."

The truth was, he and Theo seldom interacted. When Sam came back to Leverett, Theo had made it clear from the outset that they had nothing out of the ordinary to say to each other. But if Sam was wounded by his standoffishness, he knew he had no right to be. Theo had known generations of students. It had been self-deluding of him to imagine they might somehow pick up where they'd left off.

Theo's life by then was in his classroom and in the house on Jackson Street leased to him by the school. Sometimes he had students over for conferences or the occasional end-of-term party. Mostly, though, he kept to himself. He'd become a legend, revered by generations of alumni. More than the standard-issue triple threats like Ebershof and Mastermeier, it was crusty Theo Gibson who lived on in the old boys' minds as the avatar of a Leverett education. It was him they wanted to see when they came back for reunions, though he only occasionally made a showing. He was as eccentric as ever, his hair white now and his brisk stride more of a stroll. He still smoked like a chimney, the kids still called him Smokehouse, and there was the same edge to his greeting when he met you on the path. He was still Theo Gibson, only more so—more sought after, more out of reach than ever.

"What's up with Braddock?" Darman asked at a certain point.

"I haven't heard from him in years," Sam had to admit. "I think he's in California." The truth was, he didn't know where Eddie was.

Sam was remembering a dinner in the *Harvard Lampoon*'s faux-medieval banquet hall where the coolest of the cool—satirists and cartoonists and television honchos in training—mixed and mingled at the pockmarked old refectory table on Friday nights, drinking and doing drugs till all hours. Suddenly Darman was beside him, in leather pants and a fisherman's sweater, fresh from a rehearsal of one of his plays. They sat together and got slowly plastered and Dave harangued him that he'd missed the best thing Leverett had had to offer: sex—and that he'd been a coward and an idiot not to act on his feelings for Eddie.

Sam had sat silent, too stunned to be offended, while Camel after Camel went down to ash at Darman's lips. Was he the only one who envied him the freedom he allowed himself to pursue his desires? He made it look so easy! He remembered Dave's dalliance—real or invented—with Johnny Pratt. The rest of them had cared way too much about how they were perceived, but there'd been no consequences, or so it seemed, for Dave. There was something divine—divinely wicked—about him.

How surprising it had been then to run into him on a flight from London to New York during Sam's second year at Oxford and hear him talk about a love affair that was coming to an end. Darman was out of his pouting leather-jacket Mick Jagger phase by then and into his Mike Nichols *Carnal Knowledge* phase: tan jeans, black turtleneck, and chukka boots, puffing on a Winston (new cigarette, too), the cleft in his chin more prominent than ever, not to mention his new wiseass New York accent.

"He teaches at Stanford. He has a cabin up in Sonoma and sometimes we go there for the night. He's getting married in a few weeks, to the most amazing girl. She knows exactly what's what, and she couldn't be kinder.

"The thing is, Eek, I really love him. I love waking up in the morning and running my fingers through his hair. I love sitting by the fire at night with him smoking weed. He makes me happy. I don't know what to do."

It was the first and last time Darman let Sam see him vulnerable. He was at a loss, and Sam felt for him.

Now here he was extolling his wife's beauty and talents and their jet-set art-world life.

The conversation rambled on for another hour. Albert was deft, engaging, absorbing Dave's tales from a mannerly distance and as always saying next to nothing about himself. Darman performed and proposed; Albert and Sam demurred, quibbled, backfilled before giving in and assenting.

At last they got up, embraced, kissed cheeks, and promised to get together again soon, though all of them knew it would be years and that by then they'd look very different.

TOM MOUTIS, the tutor who'd taken an awkward shine to Sam at Harvard—awkward, in that Tom was engaged to be married at the time (he came out not long after the wedding)—told Sam years later that Darman had been the first man he ever had sex with.

"I was eating lunch in the Dunster House dining room with a group of undergraduates when a gorgeous young guy suddenly sat down and started regaling us with stories about the women—and men—he was sleeping with," Tom told him.

"The next night I asked him to my room. We sat on my bed and smoked a joint and at a certain point I put my hand on his thigh. 'Are you sure this is what you want?' he asked, and I nodded silently, unable to say a word. 'I'm warning you,' he said, 'being with me is like walking on ground glass in your bare feet.'"

As Moutis told his story Sam realized that his own dalliance with Tom had been going on at the same time, more or less, as Tom's affair with Darman. And Moutis was the man Dave had told him about, the one he said he'd loved.

DEAN WAS TEACHING at the writers' conference the Poets ran every July at a lake in the northwest corner of Connecticut, and he invited Sam up to give a talk on Wordsworth. The sun-flecked waters of Lake Washining with the blue Taconic Range behind it aren't the Lake District, but they're arguably southern New England's best approximation, with a green grandeur that never fails to stun students and faculty alike.

The "students" were fellow professionals, teachers from Leverett and its sister schools who wanted to replenish their creative juices in a beautiful place and gossip about literature, the tribulations of their calling, and each other over a few drinks in the evenings. The sessions took place in an old Chautauqua-style camp with lumpy-mattressed little cabins by the lake and a central hall where the readings and lectures were presented after dinner, when the temperature had fallen a few degrees and everyone was mellow.

Sam's talk on Wordsworth and the Sublime seemed to go well enough, and afterward Dean invited him to his cabin for a nightcap.

They sat side by side on the settee on his screened porch watching the moon in the water and listened to the peepers. There was one light on somewhere in the cabin. Dean had a bottle of Famous Grouse with a tray of ice from the jittery old refrigerator and they pretty much killed it, jawing about the Romantics, the students, Boris, and their colleagues. And for the first time, Sam went into the split with Anne.

"Anne has always been kind of a goddess for me—and Sharon, too," Dean said. "But I do have to admit there've been moments when I wondered if you weren't a little light in your loafers." Dean raised his chin and grinned. "Not that it's made the slightest difference to our friendship."

All of a sudden Sam said, "Come here," and leaned over and kissed him. To his surprise, Dean responded. They kept it up for a while and Sam said, "Take off your shirt," and Dean did. Sam kissed his wide shoulders and ran his hands up and down his sculpted arms. He buried his face in Dean's armpits. He licked them and ran his fingers through Dean's surprisingly soft russet chest hair and over his rugged face with its day-old stubble—everything he'd guiltily imagined but never dreamed of actually doing.

He told Dean to take his pants off and he did that, too. He was laughing, saying, "You're insatiable, Brandt!" as Sam kissed him all over, pinching his sand-dollar nipples, taking his cock in his mouth, sucking on his low-hanging balls, slapping and biting and caressing his hairy butt, reveling in his goldenness, which was silver in the moonlight. Dean let him do whatever he wanted. He was dripping all over him, enormous with lust.

Dean laughed and they kissed and they laughed and drank some more and he looked Sam square in the eye as they did. But try as Sam did, whatever he did, Dean was never aroused.

They spent the night in Dean's single bed. Sam spooned him, with his dick between Dean's thighs and his hands in his hair. When morning came, bleary-eyed and hungover, they embraced again and Dean, with bed hair and sleep in his eyes, was incredibly beautiful to Sam.

They went out for a big, companionable breakfast at the town diner, not talking much. As they were driving back along the lake, Sam said, "Don't worry. I'm not going to fall for you. I can't even get you hard."

"You know how I've always felt about you," Dean said. "I'm glad what happened happened."

"What are you going to tell Sharon?" Sam asked.

"I'm not going to tell her anything. What happens in Taconic stays in Taconic."

"Sharon has nothing to fear from me."

"She knows that."

Sam couldn't help being a bit downcast hearing him say it, even if he knew it was true.

"And you?" Dean asked, after a pause.

"I think Anne sensed what I was feeling, maybe even before I did. But our separation was a long time in coming. It had nothing to do with anyone—except me, us.

"Were *you* aware?" he asked. "As a matter of curiosity."

"Of...this?" Dean shrugged. "I knew you liked me. And that has always meant an enormous amount."

"That's not going to change."

When they pulled up at the cabin, they sat in the car and Sam thanked him. Dean just shook his head and smiled.

And that was that. Sam sat with him at the conference later that day just like before—except he was seeing him from a new distance now. He was still Dean, still his most admirable character, still adored and, yes, desired. But he was part of Sam now somehow, metabolized beyond fantasy.

HE KNEW HE HAD TO FIND a way. What or how it would be he had no idea. But there are certain things there's no turning back from. What's that Rilke line? *You must change your life.*

He took a leave.

It was Boris's idea. "The alumni need to hear about Leverett from the horse's mouth," he said, as they were wolfing down California burgers at the Grill just before school opened. "Why don't you take a road trip this winter term, spread the Morse Code gospel far and wide? It'll do you good, and it will be fantastic for us. I'll arrange cover for your classes."

Sam jumped at his proposal. Immediately he thought of making a few detours along with way, dropping in on Olson and Kaiser and some of the others.

Who knew if he'd come back?

He met the groups that the advancement office organized in clubs or the homes of alumni in cities from Buffalo to Portland, making small talk with well-heeled doctors, self-serious lawyers, glad-handing owners of small- to medium-sized businesses—not the power elite, precisely, but they all wore their green Leverett tags with names and classes scrawled with gold Sharpies and chatted about their classmates, their

challenging but rewarding careers, and their unfailingly successful children. The photos appeared in the *Bulletin*'s summer issue.

He saw Olson in Chicago. His apartment was hung with
his intricate pictograms, restrained and idiosyncratic. Albert
had been teaching at the School of the Art Institute for nearly
thirty years and had a network of former students all over
the world. He and Clara seemed unfazed by the East Coast
distractions that had waylaid the rest of them. He was still at
it, day in and day out, as trim and energetic in late middle age
as he'd been as an eccentric eighteen-year-old, only surer of
his mission, more self-directed than ever.

Sam saw another group of individuals on the road, most
of whom had never heard of the Leverett School. They were
younger men he connected with online, guys from all kinds
of backgrounds he'd meet for drinks or dinner and maybe a
little TV, followed by surprisingly open, lighthearted, need-
ful, even passionate love. And stories, endless stories, each
different if similar in certain respects. Most of his new ac-
quaintances had little hesitancy in opening up about what
had brought them to a hotel room where for a few hours they
could set aside their external differences and share what was
most unvarnished and urgent about themselves.

Most he saw once, a couple twice. A handful he stayed
in touch with when he got home; a few eventually became
friends. What bound them was an acknowledgment of

mutual need. Thanks to them a scrim that Sam felt had always walled him off from the world dissolved once and for all. Their straightforwardness and generosity closed lifelong wounds; it centered and calmed him and gave him the sense of a future, and for a few weeks it was the most important thing in his life.

EVENTUALLY HIS RENTED CAMARO took him to the mountains east of San Diego. It can be eighty-five degrees on the coast but four thousand feet up there's snow—and in spring irises, roses, peonies, bridal wreath: an East Coast microclimate in the hills high over the great Sonoran Desert.

Sam found Eddie in a cabin outside Julian. His apple farm might have been down the road from Leverett in the old days—though with the flat facades on its building fronts Julian looks like a set out of *Wagon Train*, and the town today is mainly bakeries and real estate offices. But the treescape—mesquite, ironwood, and ponderosa pine—was entirely different from anything Sam had known before.

Eddie's hair had turned silver. He was a bit more filled out than when Sam had last seen him forty years ago, but with the same wire-rim glasses and almost the same spry step, the tight smile and coiled, arch, verging-on-exasperated tone. When they held each other, the warm, spicy scent of his flesh was exactly as Sam remembered it.

The exclaiming and taking in of what time had done to them both took a while, but eventually they settled on Ed's porch overlooking the bald yellow hills tumbling down to the invisible Pacific and got around to what Sam had come for: a settling of accounts.

"You made too much of it, my friend." Eddie was characteristically a bit heated. Sam could tell he was embarrassing him, but he kept at it.

"You were all I had, Ed. You were the world to me."

"And you to me."

"No. You had Sally."

Ed and Sally had eventually drifted from Seattle to the Bay Area, married, and divorced. Later she'd married again, to a friend of theirs, and raised a family. Ed had had other relationships, some of them long-term, but had stayed single. After a series of entrepreneurial adventures he'd settled here, at the farm.

"Sally says hi, by the way. I saw her in Santa Barbara last month and told her you were coming for a visit."

"How is she?"

"Same as ever. Best person I've ever known—next to you."

Eddie's idealizing of Sam had been his way, Sam used to think, of keeping the real him, with his inconvenient needs and desires, at arm's length.

"To tell the truth, I've had erotic dreams about you in anticipation of your visit," Eddie said.

"Is that so! If only that had been the case when we were together. Are you suggesting we do something about it?"

"Hell, no. I was imagining the slip of a boy I loved, not the pudgy gimp who's sitting on my porch."

"We're a little different, aren't we?"

Suddenly he was back in Eddie's room in Urquhart. He'd come out of the shower and was toweling off unself-consciously in front of Sam: lightly muscled, brown-skinned perfection, down to the modest penis the Greeks preferred.

"It's a shame we couldn't have loved each other, Ed," Sam needled him, mainly in jest.

"It was another time. We were other people, playing by other rules. Anyway, you're the one who's been happily married all these years."

Eddie had had a son with another woman, but he and Will weren't always in touch. His current partner, a woman named Joan, lived in a neighboring town.

"Not anymore, I'm afraid. It all came apart not long ago."

"What happened?"

"We just couldn't do it anymore—or I couldn't. And then—I found you again. Someone totally wonderful. And utterly inappropriate and unavailable."

"Not a student, I trust!"

"Eddie!" Sam was laughing. "What do you take me for? No, a colleague. A younger guy. Married with children. And entirely straight."

"Yeah, yeah. I bet he can't help giving off a vibe you can't help picking up on."

"Is that what you were doing?"

"What I remember is that I could hardly get through a day without you. I bet this guy is the same, even if he doesn't admit it."

Sam shook his head. "I don't think so."

But knowing that his desperate love for Eddie had been mutual in some way was consolation, too.

They walked out onto the lawn. The shadows were lengthening and the atmosphere had taken on the heaviness that comes with dusk over the desert. Dean's girls would be getting ready for bed out East. Soon he and Sharon would be starting their evening labors.

"One thing I've learned only recently," Sam said, "is to look for love where it's to be found. Where there's nothing that I've put in its way. It's taken me a lifetime to figure that out."

"And just where is that?"

"In very surprising, out-of-the-way places."

"But not, I trust, at the Leverett School."

"We'll just have to see!"

Sam asked him then if he ever heard from Bryden.

"Not a word since he left Leverett. Not that I'm much of a correspondent."

"Well, you *were* roommates..."

"If you can call it that. I had to get out of Hollister to get away from you!" Eddie looked at Sam reprovingly. "No one else would go near him. We had nothing in common but running. Besides, he was never around."

"Where was he?"

"Hell if I know. In the library, maybe, or chem lab. Some nights I'd hit the hay without his being back in the room. He talked in his sleep sometimes. All of a sudden he'd shout out, 'Bombs away!' or have a violent argument with his mother."

"It seems he was quite attached to Gibson."

"Now there was a memorable dude. Remember our outings to New York with Darman? They were the only respite we ever had from the Gulag."

"Yeah, until Theo had to ruin it by inviting Ron along."

"Smokehouse and T. D. Tompkins. I never understood that."

"Yes, they were quite the pair. Did you ever think they might have gotten out of line with the kids—you know, handsy?"

"T.D. had the reputation, as I recall. But Gibson? Bryden used to bellyache about him sometimes, that he took advantage, whatever that meant. But I paid him no mind. He was always unhappy about something—trying to make himself look important. But Theo was a great coach, smokes and all. I used to see them doing intervals together on the river road at daybreak every now and then when I was out biking. Giving his pupil some extra pointers, I guess. He certainly could have used them.

"No, the only one I knew who took liberties was Darman," Eddie said. "He used to nose around Pratt like a bitch in heat."

"You always said Darman was cool!"

"Cool, sure. Very sophisticated, very entertaining. But definitely not my type. And not Johnny's either."

Their talk went on all evening. Eddie grilled them steaks, which brought Sam back to the night at Ed's parents' house on the Pacific, when he'd been so despairingly in love he could hardly speak. Tonight, though, there was just their old off-kilter back-and-forth as the sharp stars took over the sky, revisiting their old conundrum.

Another few drinks later they called it a night. There was only one bed in the cabin, and Sam woke with Eddie in his arms. He watched him sleep, mouth half-open, sunk deep somewhere else, encased in the mysterious otherness he had never found a way to penetrate.

Who was Eddie? Carefully, Sam got out of the bed, went into the kitchen, and made himself a cup of coffee. He went out to the porch to watch the mist rise from the hills, understanding he would never know.

HE HAD ONE MORE VISIT to make. He took the I-8 and headed into the desert south of the Salton Sea. Enormous buttes kept materializing on the horizon, each with its own shape and color, coming for him and then just as suddenly gone. He entered Arizona at Yuma, cut north on 85 at Gila Bend, and was in Phoenix by midafternoon.

The city struck Sam as a place that had only recently risen out of the sand, its glass towers pale echoes of the primordial forms that had astounded him on the road.

Sam had invited himself to dinner with Kaiser and his second wife, Morgan. He came to collect Sam at the Days Inn by the airport in a black Mercedes 500 sedan. Suddenly, there he was: the cowlick, the oily, still-dark hair—did he dye it? Sam wondered—the distracted air, as if he wasn't quite sure why they were seeing each other.

Being with Kaiser in the desert, he immediately grasped what he couldn't have when they first knew each other: how thoroughgoing a Westerner Ray was. The flat affect of Phoenix, their stately progress across the city, the desultory pace of their conversation: all were Kaiser to a tee.

As he drove to Scottsdale, Ray reflected on living in a gated community. "We almost never leave," he said, seemingly without irony and so quietly Sam had to strain to hear him.

Kaiser's law practice, in the firm his father had once run, seemed to involve representing the insurance companies he'd once prosecuted for fraud. "I should have been a shrink," he said, "but I was too crazy." His first wife, the mother of his three children, had been a colleague in the DA's office in Provo, but he'd left public service when they divorced. He'd met Morgan, a partner in an actuarial firm downtown, at the local Presbyterian church. Ray the old radical was the only one of Sam's friends who'd found God.

Their place, which Morgan explained overlooked an eighteen-hole golf course, was furnished with her family's Garden District heirlooms. They looked a bit lost in this adobe maisonette with its Mexican terra-cotta tile floors and sliding glass doors, as if awaiting transfer elsewhere. Morgan, who was maybe a decade younger than her husband, wore her abundant red hair in a chignon and had a rambunctious laugh, which clearly animated Ray, who struck Sam as chastened, becalmed. He'd retained the dignity Sam had always admired, but he found he missed his old friend's unpredictable side, the way he'd needed to get a rise out of you, even at the cost of wounding you. Sam's Ray, he realized, had been the crazy Ray. This one felt like his afterimage. Or was he under wraps, on good behavior for Sam's visit?

At one point, he asked about Darman. Ray shook his head. Not on his radar screen.

"So. Why are you here?" he asked as they were having a brandy and soda after dinner. Morgan had excused herself to work on a report that was due in the morning.

"To see you, Ray. It's been absolutely ages."

Ray nodded patiently, waiting for Sam to come to the point.

"To tell you the truth, I needed a break," Sam said. "It's been rough going lately." He gave him the short version of his story.

Ray was gentle. "I sympathize," was all he said.

"I do have a question," Sam said. "We were in Theo Gibson's English class knob year. And I'm sure you remember our Auden seminar with Darman."

Ray nodded.

"Were you in touch with Gibson after Leverett?"

"Why do you ask?" Kaiser's demeanor, as always, was lawyerly, noncommittal.

"I'm just interested in the kind of impression he might have made."

"I see," he said, indicating he didn't. "Well, I was never one of his favorites, but I remember appreciating his edge, his originality. You could see there was substance beneath the scorn."

Sam laughed. "Did it ever cross your mind that he might have acted...inappropriately with students?""

Now it was Sam's turn to wait for Ray to respond. "I understand he got a little tight at an alumni gathering out here some years back," he finally said. "There was an awkward moment with an acquaintance of mine from the class of 1996."

"What's his name?"

"Wintersteen, Daniel Wintersteen."

Frank's roommate. "What happened?" Sam said.

"I wasn't there. But I understand he was quite upset. I think he was embarrassed, by Gibson's lack of restraint mostly. He wrote him afterward—they'd been close at Leverett, according to Danny—but he never had a response. Which I think upset him more than the incident itself. No doubt he wanted to be able to fend Gibson off and still maintain a connection.

"And you?" Ray asked. "What's your opinion? I always thought of Gibson as your protector."

"He was, in a way," Sam said. "But there was never anything untoward between us. I'm sure he could sense my virginity, my naïveté..."

"Your lack of interest..."

"That, too."

"Did you two ever talk about Braddock?" Ray asked.

Sam was taken aback by Kaiser's question. But who more than Ray, after all, had had to hear about the ins and outs of his relationship with Eddie, back in the day?

"In a roundabout way," he said. "Theo always made sure you did most of the talking. Maybe he saw me as a disciple in training. I was certainly no paragon of budding manhood like the jocks he loved tormenting."

"I won't argue with you there." Sam was relieved to see the old Ray poke through. "But why delve into all this now?"

"Some history we're trying to sort out. The Head asked me to look into it."

"Well, Krohn knows all about Gibson and Wintersteen. He talked to Danny after the incident."

"Is that so."

"Yes. They met when Danny was back at Leverett for something or other. He told me he was quite satisfied with how it went."

Suddenly Sam felt an overwhelming urge to leave. "I really appreciate your being frank with me, Ray," he said. "It's been wonderful catching up, but I think I need to get back to the hotel."

He thanked Morgan for dinner and made his excuses. Ray seemed unperturbed by the change in Sam's mood and drove him back across the city the way they'd come—a neon carnie show now, cascading in the desert night.

As they embraced in front of his hotel Sam was tempted to say, *What's wrong with this picture, Ray? You're going home to watch the news with Morgan and I'm about to have a drink with Hakim, the thirty-something computer programmer I met online this afternoon. We switched places somewhere along the line. How did that happen?*

He was tempted, yes; but he let it pass.

HE AND HAKIM, IT TURNED OUT, weren't made for each other, and after one drink they called it a night.

Sam flew home in the morning and went looking for Boris the next day—a dank, gray April Thursday. He found him in the infirmary, visiting Melissa Schaumle's daughter Caitlin, who'd sprained an ankle playing hockey.

"Welcome home, pal! How was your trip?" Boris laid his red, rough paws on Sam's upper arms. "I had fabulous reports about your events. They really ate you up!"

"It was life-changing, Boris. You have no idea. But there's something we need to discuss."

"Let's take a walk."

They left the infirmary and headed toward West Bridge. The clouds were leaden over the Halsey Hills. It was still winter in Connecticut.

"I saw my classmate Ray Kaiser in Phoenix," Sam began, looking across at Boris. "You've known about Theo for years."

"Oh, known what!" Boris stopped in the middle of the path, exasperated. "That he got a little chummy with an alumnus at a cocktail party? Listen, Sam. Theo was a lonely and no doubt unhappy guy, that's a given. He may have—no, let's say he *did* have—feelings for some of the boys. You were one of them, from everything I've heard." He stared at Sam as if maybe he was responsible for Theo's behavior. "But there's no proof he ever did anything improper to anyone."

"What happened with Wintersteen?"

They started walking again. "To be honest, it was pretty hairy there for a while," he said at last. "Danny claimed that Gibson made a pass at him in 1996, when he was a senior, and what happened in Phoenix brought it all back. The lawyers were worried the whole thing could blow up in our faces. Luckily, we kept a lid on it—at a cost of three hundred thousand dollars."

"Jesus."

"Theo denied the whole thing, of course."

"Of course. So why did you do it?"

"There was enough plausibility to Danny's story that we thought it made sense to settle—without admitting culpability, needless to say. Theo's retiring was part of the agreement."

"And he died soon thereafter."

"And he died not long thereafter."

"Did he put up a fuss?"

"He did not. But he was ready, Sam. It was time.

"Which reminds me," he said, as they reached the boarded-up boathouse and climbed onto the balcony overlooking the river. Yellow ice was still choking the rushes at the banks. "What *did* you learn in Tulsa?"

"I promised Ron I wouldn't discuss our conversation."

"There you go. Our agreement with Danny was confidential as well."

"But you've heard about Theo from at least two sources, Boris. Doesn't that concern you?"

"Who's to say what went on with Theo and Ron? Maybe an encouraging pat or a consoling hug got misinterpreted by a needy kid. Maybe it was wishful thinking on Ron's part. Maybe he led Theo on. Maybe he made the whole thing up. Or maybe Theo actually did what Bryden claimed. I've seen similar scenarios, and worse, over the years. There's just no way of knowing. There's no 'truth' here."

"You settled with Wintersteen because you knew Theo was guilty."

"I did not. Danny said Theo felt him up in the Latin study. Theo denied it. It was a standoff. Settling was a way of resolving the situation. I'd have settled with Bryden, too, if necessary. Institutions do it all the time. It's how we move forward."

"But it meant letting Theo go. One of our great teachers vanished from one day to the next. Why? Because in your heart you knew he was guilty."

"The so-called truth about Gibson seems to have become your personal crusade, Sam. Why is that? Is it a little close for comfort, maybe? I have no opinion about Theo," Boris said, as flatly as Sam had ever heard him say anything. "Because I don't have to. We had a problem. We took care of it."

"So you sacrificed him out of expediency? To resolve 'a problem' you had no opinion about?'"

Boris was silent.

"Was Theo Gibson a pedophile, Boris?" Sam said. "Did we shield a pedophile?'"

"Theo Gibson gave his life to Leverett," Boris said. "With your help we've managed to protect his reputation—and ours. That's what I'm paid to do, and I'm going to keep doing it as long as I'm Head of School."

Sam turned away from him then and trudged home alone over the clumpy, brown, still-frozen fields.

"Boris makes the trains run on time," Anne liked to say. "I just wish he had more of an idea where they were going."

WHEN SAM GOT BACK to Bixler House he called Carla.

"Welcome home," she said, deadpan. "It's been so lonely without you."

"I've got fabulous news. Boris wants to get together for a drink."

Carla guffawed. "I've been waiting years, no, decades, for this call, and wouldn't you know, when it finally comes I'm unavailable."

"I guess it'll have to be just us, then."

They agreed he'd come to her apartment after dinner.

CARLA WAS RESISTANT.

"I've told you: Theo was a loner. He never had a relation-ship with anyone, as far as I know, let alone a student," she said, stoking the embers in her fireplace.

"I'm afraid that may not be quite true," Sam said. "I've learned about at least one kid, back when I was a student."

"That was long before my time," she said. "But it doesn't fit my sense of him. He was such a prude, really, when you came right down to it."

"What can you tell me about Danny Wintersteen?"

Carla turned away. "Well. I do remember that Theo was crazy about him. He wouldn't—no, he couldn't—shut up about how full of life and...and how beautiful he was. That gangly kid! Theo would practically swoon whenever he hove into view. He used to take him down to the city for concerts and things. But is that a crime, Sam? Sure, Theo loved Danny. And maybe Danny loved him. So what?"

"So nothing. If that's as far as it went."

"So who's to say?"

"Only Danny. And apparently something he told Boris resulted in Theo's retirement."

"Are you serious?"

"With hush money paid by the school."

Carla took a hard look at Sam. She disappeared into her bedroom and returned a few minutes later with a handwritten note.

"I found this in one of Theo's books when I was packing up the house," she said.

Dear Mr. Gibson,

I'd really been looking forward to seeing you last weekend. It's been ages and a lot has transpired in the intervening years. Abby and I got married right after college and Teddy and Natalie arrived soon after. And who knew real estate could be so engrossing?

I'd hoped to catch up for old times' sake, and to find out how you are, too. I've missed you and, believe it or not, I still read Horace for a reality check, as you used to say, whenever I can—though I don't have a lot of time these days. I think about you and all I learned from you—often.

So maybe you can imagine my dismay at what occurred when we finally did see each other. I guess it was naive of me to think that bygones could simply be bygones—which makes me feel like a total chump. I don't know what it is you want from me, or what you think is appropriate between a grown man and his favorite teacher from nearly twenty years ago. You saved my life so many times, in so many ways. I guess I hoped knowing how much your encouragement and care meant to me might be enough for you.

I'm begging you, Theo, please don't destroy all the good feeling, all the love I still have for you.

D.

"Oh boy," Sam said. He went to the kitchen to freshen their drinks.

When he re-emerged he said, "How's Daphne?"

"Taking names and kicking ass as ever. Why?"

"I was just wondering how her investigative skills were developing."

A half smile dawned on Carla's face. "What do you have in mind?"

"I just wondered if she'd be interested in a little scoop."

Carla's eyes widened. "Dean always told me you were evil," she said. "And all this time I was thinking you were Mr. Go-along Charlie."

"Well, Dean knows me better than anyone."

"I believe he does," said Carla with a glint in her eye that was priceless to Sam.

He got his coat and gave her a big hug.

MR. BRANDT, WHAT'S the pathetic fallacy?"

Peter and Sam were going to be doing an independent study together on the midcentury generation of poets around Robert Lowell and John Berryman in the fall. Peter had grown by leaps and bounds in the last year under Dean's tutelage, and his poems, Sam thought, verged on being publishable:

> *You're the top*
> *You're the wide Wachusett*
> *you're de trop*
> *you can make me lose it.*

went one.

> *When do I get to be me*
> *I kept trying to mention*
> *but she was too busy*
> *performing to pay me*
> *the slightest attention*

went another.

Really not bad at all.

"The pathetic fallacy is a figure of speech, where the writer ascribes human feelings or attributes to an inanimate object. For example, in Elizabeth Bishop's 'Crusoe in England' that we read in class the other day, Robinson Crusoe, back from his island, talks about a knife he had there and how, in that extreme situation, it 'reeked of meaning, like a crucifix. / It lived.' In his feverish imagination it was transubstantiated, infused with sacred life—the way the host becomes the body of Christ in Holy Communion."

"But now, back in England, it's just an ordinary knife again."

"Right," Sam said. "Or take my favorite poem of hers, 'Sonnet':

Caught, the bubble
In the spirit-level,
a creature divided;
and the compass needle
wobbling and wavering,
undecided.
Free—the broken
thermometer's mercury
running away;
and the rainbow-bird

from the narrow bevel
of the empty mirror,
flying wherever
it feels like, gay!

"It's all pathetic fallacy, isn't it? It's the poet's conscious-
ness, reflecting back her own preoccupations onto her
surroundings."

"Her wallpaper," Peter said. "Don't we all do that? I
know I do."

"Absolutely—only maybe not quite so pointedly, so poi-
gnantly. That's what a poet can do, give us 'What oft was
thought but ne'er so well expressed' in words we can't forget.
The 'rainbow-bird'—what a great image of the poet's Techni-
color imagination. But when can it fly wherever it feels like?"

"When the mirror is empty."

"And when's that?"

"In death, I guess. When there's nobody there to see.
Like the mercury, 'running away.' Set free but lost, gone."

"The kind of freedom she's imagining doesn't really be-
long to this world. That's the point, the tragedy. The poem
ends with images that are outside the frame of life. It was her
last poem, in fact."

"And what about 'gay'?" Peter asked. "Is Bishop telling
us something about herself?"

"She claimed she was rescuing the word from the tyranny of political correctness. What do you think?"

"I think she was giving voice to something she didn't have another way of expressing."

"Another metaphor?"

"Bingo!"

BORIS ANNOUNCED HIS RETIREMENT that spring, a few weeks after the *Hartford Courant* reported that the Leverett School had authorized a cash payment in 2005 to an unnamed alumnus in connection with an allegation of harassment by a former faculty member. Lizzie, it turned out, had had an offer she couldn't refuse from the University of Delaware Law School. Encomiums poured in from all over the country. Boris was winning praise for giving up his career for the sake of his spouse.

One of the leading candidates to replace him was Carla's ex, Emil Higgins, who'd been a stellar dean of the faculty at Saint Savior. Carla supported his candidacy, even if she was less than complimentary about his performance as a husband.

"That man does not understand the concept of fidelity," she'd say, shaking her head in lament, though Emil had been happily married to Denise James for over twenty years.

"Maybe it was fidelity to *you* that was the problem," Dean would answer, which always elicited a rueful laugh from Carla. When Emil came to school for his candidate's interview, she had a big party for him and Denise, and no one seemed to have a better time than Boris. It seemed a foregone conclusion that the job was Emil's if he wanted it. Melissa Schaumle's term as president of the trustees would be up next year, too, and a lot of the faculty were rooting for Marie Peterson, executive director of the Head Start Foundation, to become the trustees' first leader of color. Together, Emil and Marie would shake Leverett up in ways no one could even conceive, which it clearly needed. At fifty thousand dollars or more a year, boarding schools were no longer a middle-class option—if there still was a middle class in George Bush's America. A lot of the New Guard thought the place should get out ahead of the competition and become tuition-free. A Leverett education once again should be not about where you came from but who you became while you were here—and how you made use of the privilege afterward.

Dean, meanwhile, had been appointed chairman of the English department and Deputy Head of School at Mount Moriah. The Harris girls were applying to the Leverett class of 2012, though, and if all went well their parents would be on campus frequently. The Poets were devastated but they were doing their best to absorb the loss and prospecting for new members.

"I couldn't be prouder," Sam told Dean over lunch at the Rust Bucket. "I've always known you were a leader. But where does that leave the rest of us?" *I know we'll survive without you*, he told himself. *I just don't know how.*

"I wouldn't worry, Sam," Dean said. "Someone always comes along."

FRANK AND ELEANOR and the boys called on his birthday. Frank stayed on after the rest of them got off the line and told him, "I asked Danny about Theo Gibson. He said to tell you he was the best teacher he ever had, bar none. He thinks about him all the time and wouldn't be surprised if you do, too."

"Good to know," Sam answered. "Tell him he's absolutely right."

BORIS RECEIVED A LETTER from Ron Bryden's lawyer with a check for $65,000 to establish a fund to improve the lives of male students from the Southwest in their first year at Leverett. The terms of the gift struck Sam as excessively narrow, but Boris accepted it with gratitude and awarded Ron an honorary diploma.

He came to graduation with his new wife, Patricia, and Boris asked Sam to take them out for a celebratory lunch at the Inn.

"It's good to see you here again," Sam said.

"Just like the old days, eh, old friend?" Ron answered. "I always knew we were two peas in a pod."

DAPHNE HOMANS WON A MORSE SCHOLARSHIP, the school's highest honor, which was awarded by the faculty. She and Abby were going to Stanford. They refused to shake Boris's hand when he gave them their diplomas, for which Sam and Carla silently cheered them.

SAM STOPPED INTO MAIN on Boris's last day on the job. He was an old roué, but he'd been their roué, after all—or Sam's, anyway. Whatever his failings, he'd done an enormous amount for Leverett, and undeniably, for him.

"Wilmington, here we come," Sam said, as they sipped one more latte, prepared by Jeanne in the kitchenette next to her office.

Boris smiled his long, wide smile, masking the animus he must have felt. "Best fox hunting in the country. Longest growing season north of Washington. We're raring to go."

Soon he'd have his fingers in all sorts of pies, as chairman of the local Democratic Party, or head of the school board. Still, Sam thought he detected sadness, or something else, maybe, in those ever-mobile eyes.

"Thanks for everything, and especially for your friendship," he said, not insincerely. The fact that he was still here, that Anne and he in spite of everything were still members of what for all its flaws and foibles was a family—a backbiting, contentious, but broad-shouldered and enduring family—was largely Boris's doing.

"Sam, Leverett wouldn't be Leverett without you—and Anne, too. Home fires burning," he said. They locked eyes—his were red-rimmed, steely, while Sam's hazed over a little before he turned away. Sam put his arm around Boris and walked out of his office for the last time. The Krohn era was over.

But the Brandt years were continuing—at least until Emil decided otherwise. The Leverett School, two hundred and fifty years and counting, was turning over a new leaf. He wanted to be part of it.

AT ONE OF THEIR CATCH-UP DINNERS Sam asked Anne, "Remember when Danny Wintersteen was practically living with us Frank's senior year?"

"Such an adorable boy, braces and all. He just cried out for mothering—the polar opposite of Frank. That must have been the key to their friendship."

"I gather he's toughened up in the meanwhile."

"Frank tells me he's become a real estate mogul out West."

"You always said Leverett knows how to turn out a well-done piece of beef."

"Was I wrong?"

"Darling, you're never wrong."

Raised eyebrows. Bright eyes over the coffee cup.

"By the way, did I ever ask you what you thought of Theo Gibson?" Sam said.

"I thought he was fishy. Fishy and funny."

"Funny ha-ha or funny weird?"

"I don't know. Both, maybe."

AND CARLA WAS BACK at work on her novel.

"Could I interest you in looking at a few chapters?" she asked over an old-fashioned at the Rust Bucket. After Dean moved to Mount Moriah, Sam had kept up the old tradition with Carla.

Sam told her there was nothing he'd enjoy more.

THERE WAS SOMEONE he was crazy about. Alfie Rawls was an associate professor of classics at Trinity in Hartford. They'd met online. Joshua had told him you should let the younger ones approach you. He'd taken his advice and he hadn't been disappointed.

Alfie didn't come to campus all that often, but when he did he might have been mistaken for one of the younger instructors, maybe a bit edgier and more self-assured. Not many of them had tats, for instance, though some of the younger guys had been known to sport an earring, or even two.

He loved many things about Alfie. He loved his self-accepting nature, his deadpan humor and disabused intelligence, for Alfie suffered no fools; when he went quiet around someone you knew that person was toast. One of Sam's nicknames for him was Tech Support, and Sam was grateful for his effortless digital savvy. He loved his furry beauty, and he loved that he was a man. It was wonderful to be with someone so much clearer-seeing and less conflicted than he'd been at Alfie's age—though Alf had depths and shadows of his own that Sam was only beginning to plumb. What their relationship meant to him was something that Sam pondered at length, but Alfie had never made him feel that what they were engaged in was any less charged and meaningful for him than it was for Sam.

When they ran into Anne, she was bright. "Beautiful woman," was all Alfie said the first time they met. Frank and Eleanor were good with him, too, and he was an instant hit with the boys. And Dean gave his seal of approval when they ran into him and Sharon and Carla and the rest of the Poets, with a vanful of English 440 students, at Louise Glück's reading at the Atheneum.

"You're a lucky bastard," Dean said, as they were waiting to pee at intermission.

"I know. I don't deserve him," Sam said, sheepish.

"That's why you're a lucky bastard."

ONE NIGHT, while they were lounging on the couch in his study, Sam took his Leverett class of 1967 *School Book* off the shelf and showed it to Alf.

"Translate this for me, will you?" he said.

"*Cuius preti amor?*" Alf read aloud. "*Rebus in supremis est maximi summique esse quam se ut distribuere possit omnibus partes quasi cordis ipsius.*"

Alfie stared at Theo's jagged penmanship and his drawing of himself as a dragon with smoke coming out of his ears. Finally he asked, "What is this?"

"Something one of my teachers wrote me at graduation. I never bothered to try and figure it out."

He shrugged and started translating.

"'What price love? In the end—in the final analysis—the greatest and noblest thing is to be able to give, to share a piece of your heart with everyone.'"

Alfie handed back the yearbook. "Weird," he said.

Yes, weird, Sam agreed silently.

He still couldn't make up his mind about Theo. What had he been trying to say to him all those years ago? Was he offering noble sentiments to live by, the way people do in yearbooks? Was it an apologia, his personal credo? Or had his message been more personal, meant for Sam alone?

Part of him still saw Gibson as the Pied Piper he'd idolized as a student: the keeper of the pedagogic flame who'd given his life to his students and inspired others, Sam included, to follow in his footsteps.

Sam still felt for Theo's punishing inhuman solitude.

And what about Ron Bryden? Had Theo's loneliness become so unbearable that out of desperation he'd given in to a need he'd always been tormented by—which, if anything, had only deepened his aloneness? Desire in itself was not a crime—the Church itself said as much, though Theo might well have believed otherwise, given who he was. Did he see himself as damned by his own nature? Had the awful daring of a moment's surrender cast him into an abyss there was no escape from?

And there was Danny, too, all those years later. And Dean—and himself, for that matter. And what else?

What had Theo been after? What had he done?

And what did it say about Sam's feeling or lack of feeling for Theo that he'd chosen not to read his message all these years? Had Boris been right? Was Sam haunted by Gibson because he feared that but for the grace of God it might have been him?

He lay awake till near dawn and woke no closer to making sense of Theo's words, or to parsing him.

Listen to this Mr. Brandt," said Peter, a little breathlessly.

The moon rose over the bay. I had a lot of feelings.

I am taken with the hot animal
of my skin, grateful to swing my limbs

and have them move as I intend, though
my knee, though my shoulder, though something
is torn or tearing. Today, a dozen squid, dead

on the harbor beach: one mostly buried,
one with skin empty as a shell and hollow

feeling, and, though the tentacles look soft,
I do not touch them. I imagine they
were startled to find themselves in the sun.

I imagine the tide simply went out
without them. I imagine they cannot

feel the black flies charting the raised hills
of their eyes. I write my name in the sand:
Donika Kelly. I watch eighteen seagulls

skim the sandbar and lift low in the sky.
I pick up a pebble that looks like a green egg.

To the ditch lily I say I am in love.
To the Jeep parked haphazardly on the narrow
street I am in love. To the roses, white

petals rimmed brown, to the yellow lined
pavement, to the house trimmed in gold I am

in love. I shout with the rough calculus
of walking. Just let me find my way back,
let me move like a tide come in.

"I love how she says she wants to 'move like a tide come in.'"

"What do you think she means, this Donika Kelly?"

"I think she wants to feel that she's part of nature. She's in love and she wants to experience the inexorable pull of the rhythm of the world."

"Well said."

"When does it happen, Mr. Brandt?" Peter asked. "It's what I want, too. So badly."

"Don't worry, son. It happens when it happens. Any day now."

"I'm so ready I can taste it."

"It'll come when you least expect it. And when it does, as someone told me once, Carpe diem. Don't hold back. Don't make the same mistakes I did. Make your own."

"You're a peach, Mr. Brandt."

"Still in the fruit supermarket, eh, with all those penumbras?"

"Yes, sir. Still shopping for images."

"Well, happy hunting, Peter. I know you'll find them."

JUNE
2017

Fifty-seven members of the class of 1967, the last Leverett year to be all boys, showed up for our fiftieth reunion, some with spouses, others on their own, for a weekend of games and panels, schmoozing and drinking.

I've never been a fan of reunions, no doubt because my father was so gung-ho about them. Early on it's the athletes who dominate, who believe—and the rest of us do, too—that the school is their oyster. Over time, though, the jocks' war wounds become debilitating and we all end up hobbling around more or less the same. And everyone's kind to each other. The guys who reviled me as a dweeb at fourteen greet me like a long-lost friend, and maybe I am. Hoagie Langhorne, for one, could not be more solicitous.

But Eddie and Ray and Albert weren't here. They never come to reunions.

One person who was in attendance, if briefly, was Carla Van Ness, who's an honorary member of our class and a whole slew of others. She and Myra flew over from the Vineyard and Carla gave a standing-room-only reading, complete with foot-stomping ovation, from *Shade on the Lawn*, volume three in her Fort Worth Trilogy, which is currently sitting on top of the *New York Times* bestseller list. The Fort Worth novels, about a pair of twins growing up poor and Black in Texas in the forties and fifties, were acquired by Carla's and my old student Peter Reno, who's now an editor at Pine Street Books, and have become a certifiable literary sensation. In *Shade*, Carol, the older sister, takes a job teaching at a venerable New England boarding school. Predictably, mayhem ensues.

"It's going to be a new world around here, what with Emil going to the Ford Foundation and Dean Harris coming back as Head," said Joan Pratt, formerly Johnny, wearing spike heels and a lemon-yellow frock, as we sipped Aegean tea, the official fiftieth reunion cocktail, at our farewell party. "Old Leverett's going to be seeing some major changes."

"Yes, but Emil has done a fantastic job for us," said Jim Sobiloff, still rail-thin with a shapely silver goatee. "We've got a lot to be grateful for. I hope people keep that in mind."

They all moved on to more mixing. I had a date at the Inn. *That's not how it works, Jim,* I told myself as I made my way down School Street. *They'll forget Emil soon enough, and Boris, and Dean, and the rest of us.* It was the idea of Leverett itself—and maybe Morse Code, God help us, and Carla Van Ness—that would live on, at least for a while.

I found Darman in the bar. He's the only one of us who enjoys reunions. He used to talk about the erotic charge he got playing golf with the jocks. It was winning, really: Darman the vainglorious, our Byron, our Hamlet, had always secretly wanted to be one of the guys. And they'd been only too delighted to welcome him in. Maybe they hoped a bit of his bad-boy charisma would rub off and make them rakish by association.

He was drinking alone. He looked pretty good in an untucked old blue Brooks Brothers button-down, white jeans, and sockless Gucci loafers, though he, too, was heavier than when we'd last seen each other. He'd gotten married again, he told me, to one of his boyfriends from his days in summer stock, the same year, it turned out, as Alf and I. They were living in Sea Cliff, on Long Island. Jeremy was still stage-managing off Broadway, but Dave was more or less retired.

I ordered another gin and tonic and we got to reminiscing. The alcohol loosened my tongue and I found myself asking, "Remember that night at the *Lampoon* when you told me I'd missed the best thing Leverett had to offer? Remember what you said it was—the sex?"

"I can't say I do." Darman was slurring his words the way he did way back when. "I'm sure I was stoned out of my mind. But I'll take your word for it."

I thought then of my old Harvard pal Tom Moutis and how Darman had warned him that being with him was like walking on ground glass in your bare feet. It brought back how seductive, how intimidatingly free, Dave had always been. Some of that aura still clung to him, even now. I remembered, too, that you could never believe half of what he said—or half but no more. Darman was an exaggerator, a mythomane: not an outright liar, no, but absolutely an embroiderer.

I'd always wanted to know about his relationship with Paul Pleyel but couldn't figure out how to work it into the conversation. Finally, I just came out and asked.

"Paul, Paul," he said. "Paul was one of the most exuberant, most generous, most alive men I've ever known. And he loved my ass. And not just mine, but anyone else's he could get his hands on. That was an incredible ride while it lasted. I've never known anyone hungrier for love of all kinds, anyone freer."

How did it sit with Sandy? I wondered.

"Sandy turned the other cheek. What else could he do? You know there was no one Paul adored more.

"I was right about Leverett, Sam," Darman said. "I had a lot: Kasmin and Santino and Morton, Horton, and Pratt—and a three-way once with Blaustein and Tabor. And Anspach and Gerlach were in love, though I don't think they ever did it. It. It. Everyone thinks bro sex is such a game changer, such a definitive thing, but it's just a dick in the hand or the mouth or the butt—a couple of dicks and some back-and-forth and a lot of cum. And a lot of fun. Everyone does it alone. It's so much better with a friend. What the fuss? It's no biggie.

"And it wasn't just the kids. There was T.D., and Howie Albert—but that was after graduation so I guess it doesn't count. And Smokehouse, of course, though it was never all that great. Remember how the nicotine oozed out of his pores? And I mean everywhere."

"Theo?" I cried, in spite of myself. "How did it happen? Did he proposition you, or . . . ?"

Darman took another swig of his Negroni.

"What's the matter? Don't tell me you're still jealous after all these years. Still wishing he'd gone after you?"

"He did once, sort of, at least I thought so. But that was later on. And besides, nothing happened."

Darman raised an eyebrow. "Well, it did with us. He was standoffish at the beginning. I had to be pretty forward, but eventually he loosened up and got the hang of it. He'd come up to me in his little living room under the eaves and put his hand on my fly. And get down on his knees without so much as a by-your-leave. I was pretty light-headed walking home, I can tell you, kind of veered off the path once or twice.

"Yes, you missed a lot, Sam. But I'm sure you got yours somewhere, somehow. Everybody does."

Not everybody, Dave, I said to myself. *Not everyone sorts himself out.*

"Did he do it with anyone else—you know . . . other kids?" I asked.

Darman reared back and his eyes got wide. "Well now. Isn't that for me to know and for you to find out? And what if he did? Is it any business of yours? But, yes, there were a few. One guy—Lon, Lonnie something—was absolutely insane about him."

"You don't mean Ron Bryden?"

"Yeah. That's him. Braddock's roommate. The dork."

"You're shitting me," was all I could manage.

"Don't play innocent, Brandt. Eddie knew all about it."

"I don't think so."

Darman rolled his eyes. "Have it your way. The thing was, Ron was very possessive, very needy. Theo finally had to cut him loose."

He paid for our drinks and we walked out into the late-spring dusk. We were coming up on the longest days of the year, when the light lasts till well after nine. We walked toward the Oval, past the old library with Blagden half-hidden behind it, past the theater, the chapel, and Patterson, and onto the big wide lawn that was the heart of Leverett. The white reunion tents were ghostly now; the folding chairs were stacked, ready to be hauled away in the morning.

The sky was clear and the stars were coming into view—with a few planes arrowing noiseless overhead, going who knew where.

I was still curious, still hungry.

"Did you two ever talk about it?" I asked.

Darman seemed bemused by the question. "With Gibson? What was there to talk about? He always had that big shit-eating grin on his face when he stood up and wiped his mouth with his hand. Exactly the same every time."

Every time? Was I supposed to believe Theo and Dave had a weekly assignation?

"Actually he did say something," he added after a beat. "He used to shake his head and yell, 'Bombs away!' with a big shit-eating grin on his face before he started in. I remember because it seemed so out of character." Darman chuckled and shook his head.

Bingo.

IT WAS TIME TO GO. I hugged him and planted a kiss on his broad, still wrinkle-free forehead. Darman turned back toward the Inn, lifting his right arm in benediction. I watched him amble down the fine old street under the pooled lights teeming with insects, still loose-limbed in spite of his heft. I kept on watching till he was almost invisible, his pace

unchanged, his head bobbing left and right as if he was sing-
ing to himself. From this distance he might almost have been
a schoolboy.

I was alone on the Oval. I sat at the base of the Tower and
watched the old liner go dark, stateroom by stateroom, till all
the lights were out.

I knew what would happen when I told Dean about my
conversation with Dave, as I was duty-bound to. He'd send
out a letter to the entire Leverett community—the way they
were at schools everywhere—asking if there was anything
anyone wanted to say about Theodore Gibson. Someone,
maybe years from now, would come forward with another allegation—about Theo, or Howie Albert, or Dom Dunand, or
someone else no one knew about so far. The trustees would
launch an investigation, the lawyers would go to work, and
everything would come out in excruciating detail.

Or not. Maybe Boris was right again: maybe some things
really do stay secret, even from those of us who like to think
we're in the know.

I was lying on the lawn, watching the stars spin overhead. I was looking down from the Tower through the
fresh-minted leaves. We were all up there, trying to slough
off the selves we'd been handed and become someone else:
to rise and fly where we felt like, break fully out and away.
We never could, though, try as we might. We were bound
here—glommed together like the leaves of an ancient book,

so petrified we could never be peeled apart. Not separate, not autonomous, but not one either.

That was the sad thing: neither nor. It was always neither nor. What was it the poet said?

WHETHER YOU LOVE WHAT YOU LOVE

OR LIVE IN DIVIDED CEASELESS
REVOLT AGAINST IT

WHAT YOU LOVE IS YOUR FATE

Cuius preti amor? And Theo's note was still in my *School Book* at home, waiting to be reread, reinterpreted, understood.

CREDITS